Blood in the Water

Carrie Baize

Blood in the Water

I woke up with a splitting headache and the all-too-familiar metallic tang of blood on the back of my tongue. For most folks, I guess, this would be cause for concern: an urgent trip to the doctor for diagnosis and treatment of… whatever… but not for me.

No.

I know what it means.

And there isn't a damned thing modern medicine can do about it.

If I wore a watch, I could have set it by what was going to happen next: the call would come, sending me off to fight some monster that had the bad sense to do something to get itself on the overseers' radar.

I glared at my phone as the screen lit up.

Private number.

Against my better judgement, I picked up the phone and swiped up the cracked screen to answer.

God, I hate being right.

~1~

"Who was on the phone, Mac?"

Even after more than forty years together, I'd never totally gotten used to the sound of her voice. It was a little too high and a little too melodic to be normal. Of course, I've never really had a solid frame of reference for *normal* anyway.

"Wrong number." I grumbled when I answered.

Mistake number two… since number one had been actually answering the damned phone.

Behind me, her wings flapped. It's funny how, after so many years, I can actually tell what her mood is by the way she flaps her wings… the only thing I didn't know about her mood at the moment was if she was actually gonna sting me or just start lecturing me about duty and shit.

She flapped around my head, probably intentionally letting her wing connect a few times, and settled into a space hanging a few feet in front of my face. There wasn't a whole lot about the way she was able to move that made sense, but she wasn't exactly subject to the laws of physics, either.

"I know you're tired, Mac, but you have a duty…" Her scorpion-like tail bobbed as she spoke like a disapproving old woman's wagging finger. "You have a responsibility to…"

"Damn it, Critter! Do I look like Luke fuckin Cage to you?"

Her head tilted to one side and she squinted as she examined my face. "You look like Alex McLaren to me," she said after a moment, "but I don't know who Luke Fuckincage is, so I can't really say if you look like them or not."

I chuckled and shook my head. "You know I'm gonna go, Critter," I told her. "I mean… what else can I do?"

That was part of the problem.

As tired as I was… as many times as the universe had called someone *else* to be the go-to as I'd grown older… there were things that came up that made them still call me and, like the idiot I apparently am, I still answer the damned phone.

I moved through the house on auto-pilot, only vaguely aware that Critter had landed on the floor and was padding along beside me or even that I was working my way through the pre-monster-hunt checklist that had been burned into my brain in my very early teens. I gathered my standard arsenal: weapons from a couple different centuries and a couple handfuls of normally useful magical trinkets but, when I opened the last chest, something was missing.

"Critter?"

"Yes, Mac?"

"Where's the Ubojica?"

Critter rose up on her back paws and set her front paws on the edge of the chest before craning her neck to peer inside. "It's not here," she mused.

"No shit it's not here," I snapped. "Where the hell is it?"

"How should I know? I can't wield it!" Critter dropped her paws back on the floor and started walking toward the hall. "Maybe check the last place you passed out drunk?"

Ouch.

"You sound like Stef," I grumbled as I followed her advice and walked toward the den.

Letting Stefanie's memory in was a mistake when I needed to get focused to head out and I knew it but that didn't stop her smile from lighting up my mind or the echo of the sound of my name on her lips from catching my breath in my throat.

"Don't do this, you idiot," I ordered myself. "Not now."

I never was any good at taking orders, though.

My hands were starting to shake and the cold pit that always grew in my stomach when I thought about her was already making me nauseous. I fell into my chair and dropped my arm over the side, reaching around blindly until my fingers closed around the cold glass bottle. I closed my eyes, grateful the bottle was where I'd left it, lifted it to my lips and turned it up.

Nothing.

I scowled at the bottle. It was empty.

I must have growled or yelled or cussed or something because Critter was rushing through the door before I actually threw the bottle across the room. The bottle hit the wall, leaving a dent and crack in the drywall, and bounced back toward me a few feet before falling to the floor.

"Can't even break a fuckin whiskey bottle anymore," I muttered as I set my elbows on my knees and dropped my head. Critter stood on her hind legs and set one paw on my shoulder as my eyes slowly focused on the hilt of the Ubojica, sitting on the floor under the table in front of me.

The last place I'd passed out drunk.

"I'm too old for this shit."

~2~

Sammy was riding his bike up the sidewalk when I walked out the front door and a wave of panic washed over me as I tried to remember if I had a date with my nephew I'd somehow managed to forget.

"Ti!" he called excitedly, dropping his bike on the lawn as he rushed toward me. "I got it! I got it!"

"Great, man," I laughed as his arms wrapped around me. I gave him a hug and ruffled his hair. "Got what?"

"Pack three!" He took a step back and looked up at me grinning wildly. "Now we can..."

"As soon as I get home," I interrupted, "I'll download it."

"Can we be the Turtles tonight?" Sammy asked quickly.

"If I'm home early enough, yeah," I laughed. "Just one thing..."

"Yes, Ti?"

"Dibs on Raph," I said with a wink.

My mother-in-law thought a boy his age should be outside playing soccer or learning how to work on cars or chasing girls, but none of that was Sammy's speed. The kid was a lot like I was at his age. He was into comics and video games and bored with school because it was all too damned easy. I'd bought him *Injustice 2* for this last birthday and he'd been squirreling away money to grab the DLCs when he could.

"Imma kick your shell, Ti," Sammy grinned.

"Yeah, we'll see about that," I laughed. "Toss your bike in the truck, bud. I'll give you a ride home."

I dropped the tailgate on the truck as Sammy walked his bike over. I considered lifting it into the bed myself but decided against it. Sammy had spent much of the summer with me in my weight room and I didn't think he'd lost it all in the few weeks since school started back up. I found out about halfway through the summer that it was the compromise he'd brokered with his grandmother: if he came and worked out with me, she would leave him alone about getting involved in some summer sports program. He would ride over and work out with me and the whole time we'd talk comics and games: he got my mother-in-law off his back and I got company that wasn't Critter. It was a win-win, really.

He struggled a bit but got the bike in the bed and pushed the tailgate into place.

"You gotta get back in the gym, son," I teased.

"Lemme get the hang of my physics class, Ti," Sammy laughed.

"Fair enough." There wasn't much my mother-in-law and I agreed on… especially when it came to what was good for Sammy. The one thing we were always united on, though, was the importance of education. The kid was seriously brilliant, after all, and there was no way anyone in his life was going to let him waste it.

The short ride to his place was quiet but I knew it wouldn't last.

"You wanna come in, Ti?" Sammy asked as I turned onto the street. "Say hi to Mom and Nana?"

I'd avoided the house as much as possible over the last couple years: only getting out of my truck to help Sammy carry something to the garage and, twice, when he asked me to come to his birthday party, I actually went inside.

"No one blames you, you know," Sammy said quietly.

"I wish that were true, bud."

"Ti, I…"

"Don't forget to watch the chat." It was easier to interrupt him than have him start apologizing for upsetting me. "I'll try to get home early enough for us to play tonight."

I waited at the curb until Sammy had disappeared behind the back fence. I could see my sister-in-law glaring at my truck through the kitchen window. I think Sammy wanted to believe they didn't blame me… hell, maybe they'd even lied and told him they didn't. And maybe, somehow, he was right and they actually didn't blame me… but I still did and there wasn't much that was going to change that.

~3~

Now that Sammy was safely home, I could focus again.

Or try to.

I kinda just wanted to stop by the liquor store, head back home, and drink so much I forgot the damned phone call.

I'd tried that a few times before, though, and it never worked. The headaches would get worse, the taste of blood would turn to coughing up blood, and the phone calls would just keep coming. I'd even tried getting rid of the phone: barely cracked the screen when I set it under my front tire and backed out of the driveway.

Nothing had worked and nothing would work.

Somewhere along the line, the cosmic forces that decide who gets to save the world lost sight of what makes a good savior or something.

I was past my prime.

I'd been retired.

The next one - a guy named Jake or something - lasted three calls before he ended up in a straight jacket. So, they called me while they called the next one: a girl named Madison that managed to make it through six incidents before she drove her cute little convertible over the edge of the dam...

There'd been seven, in all, so far; the most recent one had been slaughtered on his first mission.

At some point, they'd figure out what they were doing wrong and call someone who was actually capable of taking over... I just hope they figure it out before I'm dead, too.

"Just get it done."

Yes. I talk to myself. Out loud. And you would, too, if you'd had to deal with the shit I've dealt with.

I should have driven straight to the group home the call had directed me to but, instead, I took a quick left onto Bradshaw and drove toward the beach. The call had been vague, as usual, but I was already pretty sure what I'd be facing when I got to the home and I was going to need more magic than I had on me.

See... truth be told... I'm really kind of a shit witch. Not for lack of trying, mind you. I studied it all and learned everything anyone involved with me was able to teach... I just don't have whatever *it* is that makes the shit actually work. But there are ways around everything, and I was pulling up at the beach house residence of the absolute best way I'd found to level out that particular playing field.

I parked and stepped out of the truck. My boots crunched on the gravel and picked up a few pieces that clicked against the paving stones that lined the walk to the front door. I stopped a few stones away and knelt to untie my boots. When I looked up, Coralia was standing in the now-open doorway smiling down at me. She wore a long blue dress with a flowing skirt and a silver belt: the same thing I'd always seen her wear in the house.

"You have a problem," she said softly.

I laughed. "Many. Which one do you see today?"

She smiled but didn't laugh with me which, honestly, was more than a little disheartening.

"I can't quite place it," she said seriously. "Be careful, Alex."

I nodded. Coralia knew things. I needed her to know I took her warning seriously. "Is he home?"

Now, at least, she laughed softly. "Where else would he be?"

I followed her inside, fascinated by her damned dress. As always. The way the skirt swished around her feet made it look like she was walking through water. It all made perfect sense, of course, but that didn't change the fact that she was... well... captivating is the only word I can come up with that even comes close. Which also makes sense, all things considered.

"Alex!" Nikolai's arm wrapped around my chest. "*Otprysk!*[1] What are you doing here?"

We embraced. There aren't many people I share this level of intimacy with for what seem like millions of reasons, but Nikolai and Coralia knew me better than just about anyone and, after the chill in the air at my in-law's place, it felt damned nice to be accepted for a minute.

"Nightmares," I answered as we stepped apart.

"Yours?"

"I wish."

----

[1] Child, offspring

"And you don't know for certain what you are dealing with?" He turned and walked across his workshop, collecting things as he walked through the room. This was the Nikolai I'd come to see: one of the most skilled witches in the hemisphere and one of the only people I could count on not to question my motives or methods. My relationship with Nikolai and Coralia was the main reason being a shit witch was never a problem for me: between the trinkets Nikolai enchanted for me and Coralia's protection charms, I was able to do pretty much whatever I needed, whenever I needed.

I shrugged even though Nikolai's back was toward me. "Feels kinda like a cauchemar, from the call."

Nikolai stopped what he was doing and glanced back over his shoulder with a familiar sparkle in his eye. "Really?"

If there was one drawback to having a witch friend charge trinkets for you, it was that you usually ended up collecting bizarre ingredients for them in return. I could tell by the look on his face that he had a list of bits for me to collect from the creature if it was, in fact, what I thought it was.

"Because if it is…"

"Either gimme a list or a bag," I interrupted.

Nikolai nodded and turned back to the worktable. I knew better than to interrupt *while* he was working, so I amused myself by examining some of the prepared charms on the table and what was left of some of the other creatures I'd brought back to him over the years. The latter really wasn't as cool as it sounds: for the most part I was just looking at a bunch of jars and boxes. Sometimes, something in one of the jars would move a little… but that was all the excitement the ingredients could manage. The trinkets were always fun, though: tiny ceramic spiders that wrapped targets in nearly unbreakable webbing, buttons from a thrift-store medic's uniform that held healing spells, and small acrylic cubes with tiny figures suspended inside that…

"Why did they call you?" Coralia's voice interrupted from few feet up the hall.

"Why not?" I'd been asking myself the same thing on the way over, when I wasn't kicking myself over losing Stefanie that is. It didn't make a hell of a lot of sense to pull me out of mothballs to deal with, what amounted to, a pretty run of the mill call: even if it was a rare creature.

"Come here, child," Coralia said quietly.

I couldn't have argued even if I wanted to and there was a corner of my mind that always wondered if she didn't drop a bit of siren song in the mix when she didn't want to be challenged. Not that it mattered: I was already walking back up the hall to where she was standing.

She took my hands and we locked eyes. Okay: that's another wild understatement. Honestly, though, everything is when it comes to Coralia and her magic. We didn't just lock eyes: she kinda trapped me with hers and looked so deeply into my soul that she was probably able to see my last three lives.

"Something is very wrong with this whole situation, Alex," she said softly. "Listen very closely to my voice. Be sure you come back to us."

I don't know exactly what she did, but I felt it… there's just no way to explain it, though. Whatever the actual effect of her words, the bottom line was that I felt about fifty times more likely to get out of whatever shit I was about to get into… and, if things were as dire as she believed and as out-of-whack as they felt, I was going to need all the help I could get.

Nikolai turned toward us with a pile of stones and charms in his hand and an extremely concerned look. "What do you know, *lyubov*?"

"Nothing," Coralia said softly. "That's what concerns me."

Nikolai nodded as he approached us. He held out the new trinkets and stood there, nervously tapping one heel on the floor while I collected the small arsenal and stashed it in my various pockets. He was looking very intently at me: reading my aura. While most people don't even realize it's being done, to me it was an uncomfortable and disturbingly invasive experience and there had been some pretty terrible consequences for people who had tried to do it without permission… but Nikolai and Coralia were the exceptions.

"What do you see, old man?" I asked after a moment.

"Nothing to worry about, Alex."

I nodded, kissed them both on their cheeks, and left the house. In all the years they'd been a part of my life, the three of us had never said goodbye when we parted ways and, in spite of their obvious concerns about this particular call, we weren't about to start. On top of that, Nikolai was as good a liar as I was a witch, but he'd never said or done anything that could cause me any sort of harm. I had to trust that whatever he saw was something he believed I could handle.

~4~

I drove to the group home that was suffering. Multiple residents, I'd been informed, had reported the same nightmare over the last few weeks: waking struggling to breathe with a hideously misshapen creature crouched on their chest. The first few attacks had been dismissed by staff: written off as nothing more than your normal nightmare, possibly paired with anxiety symptoms caused or exacerbated by fear. It wasn't until nearly every resident had been attacked at least once that the severity of the situation was elevated to a level that caught the overseers' eyes and, subsequently, led to the call.

Maybe that was why they called me, I decided as I parked next to the home's battered blue van. They let it go too long and now the damned thing was too strong for the kid that was supposed to be doing this job. I guess calling me was better than losing another one. Especially since the whole damned council had sat idly by and watched as I transformed from their only real long-term success to a rudderless vaguely human-shaped pile of anger with almost nothing left to lose. And eventually, even the overseers would realize I was simply too old to continue being drafted back into service, right?

I walked up to the front door and rang the bell. I'd been to places like this before and I knew the protocols.

I had to wait to be admitted.

I would only be allowed to talk to the staff unless they decided to allow me access to the residents.

And if they *did* decide to do so, any conversation I had would take place under the supervision of a likely-skeptical staff member.

And that was all only if things went well.

The gal that answered the door looked at me like I was the last person in the world she expected to see. Or wanted to, for that matter. "Can I help you?" She sounded frustrated and exhausted.

I stuck out my hand and nodded. "Alex McLaren," I introduced myself. "I'm here to help with the nightmare problem."

Her eyes narrowed. "Really?" It was hard to tell what was going on in her head: either she didn't believe I was there to help, or she didn't think I could. In her defense, though, she was probably expecting a shrink and they normally don't show up in jump boots, jeans, and bomber jackets. "Look, I'm sorry, mmm…"

"Mac's fine," I offered. I could tell it bugged her not to be able to address me in a manner *she* felt was proper, but I simply couldn't provide her with what she was looking for. "Really."

"We insist our residents speak to authority figures formally," she informed me with a sneer. "We couldn't possibly allow them to be so familiar with you."

This was seriously one of the worst things about places like this. There wasn't much in the way of oversight once they got set up and the actual regulations were quickly supplanted by, what was almost always, a set of severely outdated moral and behavioral expectations. It was like getting a government check for each person they supposedly cared for somehow completely erased seventy-five years of social advancement.

"I'm sorry you feel that way." Bitch. "But you called for help and I'm the one that got sent. If you'd rather try to continue dealing with this on your own, then I'll just…"

"I didn't mean to offend you," she interrupted. I resisted the urge to explain to her the difference between annoy and offend, how improbable that really was, and just what would have happened if she *had* somehow managed to offend me. "But you're really not who I expected they'd send."

"I'm never the one people expect will be sent." I shrugged. "Occupational hazard," I added with a smirk. "Now, you wanna fill me in on what's been going on?"

She nodded and waved me inside. I wish I hadn't anticipated the chilly reception but the fact of the matter was simple: this area was about fifty years behind the rest of the country socially and, when you figured the country itself was ten years behind the rest of the world, the fact that acceptance and tolerance were just words on a spelling test to these folks it really wasn't a huge surprise. Thankfully, what they think of me has jack to do with why I'm here or my ability to get the job done.

The gatekeeper led me to a small cramped office: the room was dominated by a desk that had to have been brought in in pieces and a collection of metal file cabinets, complete with rusty corners where the faded avocado green finish had chipped off probably thirty years earlier.

"Please…" She waved toward a chair facing the desk that had probably matched the file cabinets sometime in the last couple decades.

I sat as she walked around the desk. I might have found her attractive in another life: slender without being skinny, with soft curls and bright eyes… but the permanent scowl and the way she sneered when she spoke turned me off. Nevermind the fact that I'm pretty sure those oh-so-charming elements didn't show up much unless she was forced to interact with someone that triggered all her biases. Y'know… like now.

"It started about a month ago, mmmm…"

"Mac." Jesus, lady, it's not that fucking difficult.

"Mac," she repeated, nodding slowly. "Right. I'm sorry, it's just…"

"Started about a month ago?" Damn, woman, just give me the information I need so we don't have to deal with this bullshit.

"Kelly Randall," she said, nodding as she slid a folder across the desk. "Came to us about three months ago with a few severe addictions and…"

"I don't need to know what excuses you all came up with for the incidents." I probably should have been a little more polite, but the woman was already on my last nerve. "I just need to talk to the victims."

"Please don't encourage them," she said sternly. "They had nightmares, mmm… Mac. They have issues and they're disturbed, but they're not victims."

"Can I just talk to them, please?"

"Wait here," she said as she stood up. "I'll gather everyone who's complained."

The door closed and I reached for the folder. While the victims' other issues almost certainly had nothing to do with the attacks, there might be something in the data that could be useful. Other than lists of drugs the residents had been addicted to, though, there really wasn't much there. I wish it surprised me, but I was really getting the feeling that this place was only slightly better than a lockup and that the residents couldn't expect the rehabilitation the facility advertised. The only data of any use to me was the frequency of the attacks: data I already knew.

It started a month ago with Kelly Randall: attacked on three consecutive nights by a creature that crouched on her chest with such pressure that it was difficult to breathe and she thought her ribs were going to crack. On the third night, the creature moved to another resident and the cycle was repeated. If it was a cauchemar, it wasn't behaving normally. The creatures devoured and moved on: they didn't hang around establishing feeding grounds and they didn't keep their victims alive.

Something was off.

I needed more information and I wasn't going to get it from the home's files.

There wasn't much else in the office that was going to help either.

I needed to talk to the victims.

I stood up and paced the length of the ridiculously oversized desk. It wasn't terribly satisfying, nor did it really accomplish anything, but it was better than just sitting there. While I waited for the administrator to return, I replayed the events at the beach house in my mind. Nikolai had seemed pretty damned excited by the possibility of adding some cauchemar bits to his collection of ingredients but once Coralia started adding safety charms to the mix he seemed to have completely forgotten about it. It seemed that every call was making a little less sense than the last and that was a pretty sobering realization to come to… or maybe the fact that I was sober was the real problem. Hard to say, really.

I was leaning against the desk with my thumbs hooked in my belt loops when the administrator came back through the door. She glared at me, presumably because I didn't stay stuck to the avocado green naugahyde covered chair she'd left me in, then nodded. "Everyone who's complained about the nightmares is on the back patio," she told me. "I'll show you the way." This woman couldn't have shown me the way out of a paper bag, but I smiled and nodded anyway.

I followed her through the house and out the back door. There were almost a dozen folks scattered around the patio: a couple of them looked like they hadn't slept in a week and three looked like they'd been chain smoking for a year straight. Other than being stuck here for whatever reason, it was obvious the victims had little in common… other than the residual stench of having tangled with a force that didn't belong here.

The administrator introduced Kelly Randall. The girl didn't look old enough to have had the sort of problems that end up with a young woman stuck in a place like this and she seemed a little too timid for any of the scenes that might have got her wrapped up in the wrong shit. More important to the task that had been dumped in my lap, though, was that she didn't have the scar. When otherworld forces established feeding grounds here, they always mark their game. It's not a normal scar: more of a magical branding system that only some of us can see.

Kelly Randall wasn't marked.

None of them were.

I asked all the questions the administrator expected me to, analyzing the parts of the victims answers I actually needed as I moved through the group. It definitely *sounded* like cauchemar but there were a couple things that didn't quite fit and those things were what was bothering me. I needed to see inside the house.

The administrator refused, of course. I figured she would. The whole thing was just too weird for her: she didn't actually want answers or a solution, just a blanket prescription for sleeping pills to make her charges sleep through the night. I twisted the silver and lapis ring on my forefinger and nodded slowly as I extended my hand.

"I do understand the need to maintain privacy and security," I told her as we shook hands. "But I wish you'd reconsider. I really can't help your residents without being able to examine their rooms."

"That's fine, Mac," she replied with the first genuine smile I'd seen on her face since I knocked on the door. Damned shame I had to trip a charm spell to see it. "I can take you upstairs."

I followed her into the house and up a narrow staircase, listening to her ramble data about her operation that I neither wanted nor needed to know: the fact that she'd been running the house for five years, that their residents were considered some of the best cared for in the region, and that there had never been any problems like this until Kelly Randall's first complaint.

Kelly shared a room with Britteny George, the second victim. Her story was the same as Kelly's: hideous monster crouched on her chest, crushing and possibly cracking ribs. The creature moved across the hall after that, then zig-zagged its way down the corridor.

Other than the attack itself, none of it was normal cauchemar behavior. They were creatures driven by hunger: they weren't methodical or patient, and they didn't leave their prey alive long enough for people like me to be alerted to their presence. There had to be another explanation.

"I'm going to have to do a little research," I told the administrator when we reached the end of the hall. "Can I come back in the morning to take care of this?"

She smiled warmly. "Of course, Mac. You're welcome any time."

I drove home, wondering how long the charm spell would last and how much of a hassle I was in for when I went back the next morning. I had some serious work ahead of me on this one: trying to determine if it actually was cauchemar and, if it was, it why they were behaving so damned strangely. I wasn't much for the homework aspect: I've always been more of a point-me-at-a-target-and-stay-out-of-my-way type. Digging through tomes and searching through digital archives for answers really didn't do much but irritate me.

And having to work on this meant I wasn't going to be able to play with Sammy.

That pissed me off.

Critter came into the library a couple minutes after I started my research. I'd wondered where she was when I came in, but it hadn't really been a major cause for concern. There was nothing that bound her to me or forced her to stick around although, considering the asshole I can be sometimes, I know that might seem a little hard to believe. But it's true: she was the monster that lived in the shadows of my childhood closet and, because that had been the safest place for me throughout my childhood, we became friends.

"Whatcha doin, Mac?"

"Trying to figure out what the hell I've been called in for."

She jumped up onto the desk and craned her neck around the edge of the monitor then turned and scowled at me. "You smell like cauchemar."

"That's actually uncomfortably reassuring." She turned and looked at me like I'd lost my mind and, while she was probably right, I realized I had once again not even considered what might be my best source of information. "My first thought based on the complaints was cauchemar," I told her. "But it's not behaving right."

She sat on the desk, looking even more like a stuffed-animal version of her species than normal, and nodded. "Tell me." She nodded while I explained what was wrong with the situation: the systematic approach, the lack of marking, the victims surviving multiple attacks. "Something is definitely wrong," she agreed. "I should go with you."

I knew she could take care of herself - Hell, she probably had a better chance getting out of whatever shit was about to go down than I did - but that didn't mean I was comfortable with the idea of willingly taking her into a potentially dangerous situation. The overseers liked to think I was their ace in the hole - their one foot soldier that had nothing left to lose... but they were wrong. There were two things left in the world that I cared about and if either of them got hurt because of this shit the overseers had to know that the fury they relied on would be turned full force on them. Of course, at the end of the day, my feelings on the matter were irrelevant. If Critter had decided she was going that was pretty much the end of it. If I didn't willingly take her, she'd find a way...

and she knew all the best places to hide in my truck so that I wouldn't be able to find her until it was too late.

"I can probably handle it, Critter."

"Well, I'm not taking any chances." She laid next to the computer and crossed her front paws. "There's something seriously wrong with that cauchemar and I don't…"

"Slow down, Critter." She hated it when I interrupted but she'd just opened the can of worms I'd been hoping for. "Whaddya mean there's something wrong with it?"

"I'm not sure exactly what's going on with it." She sounded nervous and a little more creeped out than she should have been. "But there's something really wrong. It smells like…"

Come on, Critter. Gimme something to work with.

"Kinda like something else has got it on a leash."

"Well, that's something." The power necessary to control a cauchemar was insane and, just like that, I was way more unsure of my success than I had been a minute earlier. "Think I should stop by Nik's again?"

"Definitely seems like a good idea."

"Okay." I knew she was as protective of me as I was of her so, all things considered, I wasn't going to argue much more. "I told the admin I'd be back in the morning. I wanted to get some info and…"

"Go to sleep, Mac," Critter interrupted. "Get a good night's rest. We'll go see Nikolai and Coralia first thing and then go deal with this."

I nodded and laughed a little. "Yes, dear."

<h1 style="text-align:center">~5~</h1>

Critter's been part of my life for as long as I can remember. My childhood closet was home to a handful of creatures, but she was the one that consistently stuck around when I sought refuge there. She was the one that cared about me and worried about why I was hiding with her in the shadows. Plus, once the whole calling thing came up, she was really a pretty awesome sidekick to the whole reluctant superhero shtick.

I called her Critter when I was little because I had no clue what she was and that was what my mom called pretty much any living breathing thing that was physically smaller than her. Me included. As I got older and realized how important it was to call people by their proper name (and she'd been *people* to me for some time by that point), I asked her what she would prefer. She told me her name which, it turns out, humans are actually physically unable to pronounce but quickly added that it was perfectly fine with her if I continued to call her Critter.

She'd been with me through everything and I still find myself wondering how long before she takes off, like Elliott once Pete had a family to love him, to help some other kid who needs someone to keep them company and take care of them while they try to find a life that doesn't involve hiding who they are. I'd asked her more than a few times over the years why she continued to stick around but she'd never given me a real answer.

I didn't normally sleep well when I was in the middle of something, so the fact that I both passed out pretty much immediately and stayed asleep was basically nothing short of a minor miracle... or a side effect of having a manticore watching over you, I guess.

Critter was sitting on the nightstand, posed like a library lion, with her eyes closed when I woke up. I considered, briefly, trying to sneak out and leave her safe and comfortable in the house but I knew not only that it was almost completely unlikely to work, but that there'd be hell to pay if I tried.

"Wake up, Critter." I got out of bed and walked toward the bathroom. "If we're gonna do this, we gotta do this."

"Your eloquence is overwhelming in the morning, Mac." I watched her yawn and stretch in the mirror as the shower started to steam. She jumped down from the spot where she'd perched during the night and I stepped into the shower and pulled the door closed.

When I walked into the kitchen after my shower, Critter was on the counter fumbling a k-cup into the coffee maker while she muttered under her breath about her lack of opposable thumbs. Next to the coffee maker, there was a banana and the still packaged pieces of what would be a breakfast sandwich once I stuck them together in the microwave.

"Awwe. You made me breakfast." I couldn't help but chuckle. She was *always* on my case about adding whiskey to my coffee and trying to convince her it was breakfast. "Thanks, Critter."

"Don't patronize me, Mac." She finally managed to get the coffee maker set and slammed the button with her paw. "I won't have you going off to face some..."

"Critter." She scowled when I interrupted but the last thing I needed was the pessimism of an overly concerned miniature manticore... especially before I'd even had any coffee. "It's okay... okay? We got this."

She nodded slowly and sat down on the counter. "Seriously, Mac... this is a really bad situation."

I layered all the pieces in the ceramic stacking thing Stefanie had bought when her sister was selling kitchen gadgets and set it in the microwave. She'd used the hell out of the thing, but I don't think I'd even touched it until Critter dug it out. She'd watched Stef use it enough that she knew what to do and could manage a slightly mangled breakfast sandwich when she had to... like she did when she first pulled it out. Critter taught me how to use it when I finally sobered up enough to make sense of her instructions and since then, if she was worried that I wasn't eating enough, she'd pull out the ingredients and nag me into making something.

Maybe that was why she was worried... because I hadn't argued about it.

The microwave beeped and I dumped the contents onto the counter and reassembled the sandwich. "So..." I took a bite and grabbed the fresh cup of coffee. "Nik and Coral's then the group home, yeah?"

"Alex..."

Ouch. Critter was the one person I could count on to call me Mac no matter what... unless I was seriously majorly screwing something up, that is.

"This is extremely serious and you need to take it extremely seriously."

As often as she gave me shit about repeating myself, I decided it was probably safer not to mention the fact that she'd just done the same thing.

"I know, Critter." I set the sandwich and coffee down before looking squarely into her eyes. "Believe me, I know. The power necessary to control a cauchemar is... shit. I can't even come up with an example." And putting it all to words wasn't helping. "This is some seriously major league shit to pull a retiree off the bench for so I figure there's only two ways this can go down..."

Critter didn't say anything and I couldn't tell if that was good or bad.

"I can be myself and take this like I would anything else and pray my instincts get us through..."

"Or?"

At least she was listening.

"Or, I let it get to me and pull some dumbass rookie move that gets us both killed. Or worse."

"Okay." She walked across the counter and sat down in front of me. "Okay, I get it."

"Okay." I took a drink of coffee. "So, we're good?"

"We were never not good, Mac." It looked like she was snarling at me, but she was smiling. At least, I think she was smiling. It was kind of hard to tell. "I just needed to understand *why* you didn't seem to be taking this seriously."

I finished my breakfast and grabbed my gear. My life had never really been normal and it had gotten even less normal after I was called, but this whole situation was way out of the scope of normal even for me and I really wasn't looking forward to the possibility of having to deal with whatever had a damned cauchemar on a leash.

"Ready to roll, Critter?"

She flew around the corner, scowling at me as she struggled to maneuver through the house carrying the Ubojica. It looked like she was getting ready to bitch at me for not grabbing it, but my face must have shown just how surprised I was to see it. Of all the things I could have forgotten when I grabbed my gear, I somehow managed to leave behind the one thing that might actually save my ass if everything else failed.

"I was going to say something," Critter said as I reached out and took the sheathed blade from her grasp. "But I can see you're thinking what I was going to say, so I'll refrain."

"Yeah." I nodded as I wrapped the belt around my waist. "I'm a fuckin idiot."

"That wasn't what I was going to say."

"No." I shook my head and opened the front door for her. "But that's what whatever it was you were gonna say meant."

Critter shrugged and jumped into the truck and I just shook my head.

Stef used to say that she was really my second wife: that she'd come late into my life and Critter's word was law when it came to me... of course, they agreed on everything so it was pretty much irrelevant. In the years we'd been married, I'd wondered many times if Critter actually liked Stef or if she just tolerated her for my sake: but in a tiny fleeting window of sobriety just after the funeral, I found Critter curled up on Stef's wedding dress crying. I left her to mourn and truly realized it was more than just tolerance.

Two wives it was... my manticore and my fairy-tale princess.

At least I never had to deal with multiple mothers-in-law.

~6~

The beach house was quiet when we pulled up: a beacon of serenity amid the sea of chaos that swallowed up the normal world. I stopped to kick my boots off and Coralia pulled the door open, nodded slowly.

"More than you anticipated, Alex?"

I nodded as we walked inside. "Nightmare fuel." She glanced back over her shoulder and frowned. "Even for me."

"You do understand that that statement, particularly coming from you, isn't very reassuring."

"Sorry, *en pen*, but it's all I got."

Coralia nodded and pointed down the hall. "Go see him, Alex. *Critter*, you come with me." (Obviously, Coralia didn't call Critter *Critter* but since I can't actually say her name and Coralia can…) I nodded and walked toward Nikolai's workshop. I mean… what else was I gonna do? You don't call a magical creature *my lady* in any language and then not do what she says, right?

I was just lifting my hand to knock when Nikolai's voice came through the door. "Alex! Come!" I was pretty sure he wasn't angry, at least not at me, but he damned sure sounded like he was. I entered the workshop more carefully than I had in years: I'd almost go as far as to describe it as timidly. Don't get me wrong… I'm not afraid of Nikolai. I mean… I am… but I'd be damned stupid not to be. When I actually saw him, though, I knew he wasn't angry… he was worried. "What have you gotten yourself into, *otprysk?*"

The way he was standing… the tone of his voice… if I'd been doing a decent job of hiding my fear before, and I wasn't convinced that I was, my ability to do so just flew out the window. "I just answered the phone, Nik." My voice sounded weird to me: weak… like a little kid.

"Maybe you should have let it go to voicemail."

I wanted to laugh. In that moment, more than anything else, I just wanted to laugh at his shitty joke. But no sound would come out of my throat. All I could do was nod.

He nodded toward the worktable. "Show me what you have."

I walked across the room and obediently laid out every weapon on my person: every charm, trinket, blade, and firearm. That had gotten me in hot water with the overseers the first time they pulled me out of retirement but I hadn't budged: if they were going to continue to call me to clean up their messes, I was going to do it my way. If they didn't like it, they needed to find someone else. God, I wish that had worked.

"Your *khranitel*[2] told you this is not enough, yes?"

"She told me the only explanation for its behavior is that the cauchemar's being controlled."

"Do you understand the power it takes to keep a cauchemar?"

"I know I can't do it." It wasn't a lie and I don't think it was me just being a smartass but it's hard to say for sure. Being a smartass is kinda how I deal with shit.

"*I* can't do it." Nikolai snapped. "I can't even *call* the damned things!"

If there were ever a day *not* to be sober, today was turning into that day really quick.

"What am I gonna do, Nik?"

Nikolai smiled and nodded at the weapons on the table. "You, *otprysk*, are going to beat it."

"Excuse me?"

"You heard me."

"But you just said…"

"I know what I said, Alex." I wonder if I scowled the same way Critter does when I interrupt her. "I'm not senile yet. But I also know you. I know your strengths and what you are capable of."

"You also know I'm too old for this shit, right? That *fighting monsters is a sport for the young*?" I never really tried to mock Nikolai before, but I was just angry enough that I did a pretty good impression of his accent just then.

"You will beat it…"

I resisted the urge to point out that he was repeating himself.

"…because you must. There is no other acceptable outcome."

---

[2] Guardian

"No other acceptab...?!" I could feel my fists clench and couldn't force myself to release them. "God damn, I need a drink."

"You need to calm down, Alex." Nikolai took a step back - away from me - which was strange because he could basically wipe me from existence with a wave of his hand if he wanted to.

"Calm down?" I still couldn't unclench my fists but I managed to keep my feet stuck to the floor rather than stepping toward him. "Do you hear *any* of the fuckin words coming out of your mouth, Nik?"

"You are angry."

"Y'think?!" Was he *trying* to get me to die trying to kill him? Because that's kind of what it was feeling like.

"Harness it."

"What are you...?"

"Breathe, *otprysk.*" He opened his hands with his palms facing me. Nonthreatening. I could process that, but not much more. "Deep. Slow breaths." My brain was trying to follow Nikolai's instructions but my body didn't much want to cooperate. "You must control it for it to be of use."

"Control what?" I was really hoping my brain would be able to process whatever answer he gave me because, the way I was feeling, I didn't feel confident in my ability to process much more than my own growling. He pointed behind me toward the door and I turned and looked. I'd seen the inside of that door a thousand times and never once seen the strange writing that now covered its surface and a good portion of the wall around it. "Nik?" I really wanted to quit growling, but that didn't seem likely.

"The *domovoi*[3] is with you, *otprysk.* Sharing your body. Augmenting your strengths."

"You had your fuckin guard dog possess me?!"

"He does not possess, really..." Nikolai laughed and, thankfully, the sound finally started to melt the icy rage that had consumed me. I could move my fingers. Unclench my fists. "He's just there to give you a boost. He underestimated your strength, though."

"But you didn't." It was starting to fall into place. More than that, I was starting to feel like myself. "That's why you disarmed me."

"You are... understandably nervous, Alex. It seemed best to proceed with caution." He smiled as he added a few trinkets to the table. "I am fast for an old

---

[3] Household guardian spirit

man, but not fast enough to cast before your bullet hits, eh?" He smiled and winked.

I still wanted to be mad at him. "You could've mentioned it."

"Then you would have said no. That was not an option. You *need* his strength for this, Alex."

"I know. I just…" I still really wanted to be mad, but I was regaining control of myself and I knew Nikolai was right. "This is why Coralia kept Critter with her?"

"Partially, yes. Your *khranitel* would have done all in her power to prevent the joining."

"And the *domovoi* would have killed her."

"Most likely, yes."

"Nik?" I wanted to be furious but, in the decidedly fucked up way my life had been going, I couldn't even be properly angry. Hell, I was actually even grateful that they'd kept Critter away from me while Nik helped his rabid house elf invade my body. And I knew it was unfair to put any blame on the *domovoi*: they're actually very kind, protective beings that bind themselves to one household basically for eternity. And as far as Nik's was concerned, I was part of the family. It really was just trying to help. I could come to terms with it all, and even forgive Nikolai, if he answered my next question correctly. "Is Critter alright?"

It was clear from the look on his face that Nikolai wanted to be upset that I'd asked: maybe even angry or offended. The part of his brain that controlled his speech, though, was wise enough to understand just how betrayed and distrusting I felt just then. "She is unharmed."

Good answer… but not exactly the one I was looking for.

My hand was on the doorknob before I even fully processed what I was doing. Somewhere in the back of my mind, the tiny often-ignored voice of reason muttered something about being glad it didn't have to fight me to leave my weapons on the table. I'd be back for those, though. Right now, Critter was the priority.

I roared her name - her *actual* name - as I headed up the hall toward the front of the house. (At some point later, I'd theorize that it was the *domovoi* that actually yelled for me. The only thing that really mattered in that moment, though, was getting to her.) Deep in my gut I was certain they'd done something to her, too, and I had to see her. My feet slid a little on the tile as I turned into the kitchen and the sound of Coralia's voice. I don't even know what she was saying - just that she was speaking in my general direction and the tone may as well have been a brick wall. When I hit the doorway, I stopped dead in my tracks.

"Oh, God! What did you do?"

"Calm down, Mac," the woman standing next to Coralia said in a slightly deeper version of Critter's voice. "This was my idea."

"Wha… I…?" I could feel my head shaking back and forth but I didn't feel like I had any control of my body. Honestly, I didn't feel like I had any control of anything. I squeezed my eyes shut and opened them again, but the woman was still there: walking toward me and reaching out to take my hands.

"Calm down, Mac," she repeated.

I reached up slowly and set my hand on her cheek.

"It's just a mask," she said reassuringly. "Just so I don't have to focus on keeping a disguise up while we deal with this."

I was still shaking my head, stammering like an idiot. You have to understand, manticores are incredibly beautiful and regal creatures… even the miniature ones… and every bit of that mesmerizing, damned near ethereal beauty had been transferred to the human frame standing a few feet away from me.

"So you just…"

"I can't go in there as myself, Mac," the woman in front of me said. I was still trying to wrap my head around this woman being Critter and the thoughts I was having about her weren't helping. "And if I have to worry about keeping up a disguise, I'm no use to you."

My mind was coming up with plenty of ways this woman could be of use to me and none of them had to do with the cauchemar. I needed to focus.

"I need a drink."

"I don't know that that's such a…"

"Coralia." I turned and my finger snapped up in front of my face like I had been working on a Harrison Ford impersonation. "Don't lecture me right now. Just give me a fucking drink." I turned back to the woman, who was still standing too close and smelled faintly of cinnamon and vanilla. "What do I call you?"

The woman thought for a moment. "Milik? Harta? Istri? Pick one. I'll answer to whatever you call me."

This was so not helping. I knew the names she'd offered had to have meaning but I didn't recognize any of them and, the way my mind was working,

I was a little afraid to just pick something I couldn't translate. Nikolai put a glass in my hand and I drank it. Vodka. I held it out for more.

"Belle," I said, after drinking about half the second glass. "I'll call you Belle."

It was honest. It was easy to remember. And, if there was any goodness in the universe at all, I wouldn't fuck it up and call her something else. I finished the second glass of vodka and walked back toward the workshop without another word.

I could hear Belle and Coralia talking as I walked away and did everything in my power not to hear them. I needed my weapons and to get this cauchemar taken care of so I could go back into retirement and not have to deal with any more of this shit.

"I did not know," Nikolai's voice said from the door. "Not for sure. Coralia thought she might ask but…"

"I get it." I fastened the Ubojica's belt around my waist, holstered my pistol, and began picking up the trinkets and charms. "All you knew when I asked was that Coralia wouldn't have done anything to hurt her. And you couldn't have known if she actually asked or not because you were in here getting everything set up with the *domovoi*." I turned back toward the door and saw Nikolai standing there, nodding slowly.

"That about sums it up." He shrugged a little and grimaced. "I am sorry, Alex. You know we love you like you are our child." Nikolai lifted his hands slightly in a show of defeat. "We are just trying to help you survive this one."

He was serious. Fuck. "Is it that bad, Nik? Really?"

Nikolai nodded slowly. "I am afraid it could be, Alex."

I took a deep breath and cracked my knuckles in front of my chest. "Awesome."

Nikolai chuckled and shook his head. "You have no fear, Alex. This is what worries me." He handed me a small leather purse. "These are weapons for… you are calling her Belle, yes?"

"Yeah." I nodded and grabbed the purse strap before stepping past him into the hall.

"Be cautious," Nikolai said as I walked past him. "This situation is unlike anything else. You must be very careful."

I waved over my shoulder, hoping to silence the doomsayer mode before I got back to the kitchen and took it out on Belle.

"*Otprysk!*" I sighed and turned back around to see a limp fabric bag flying toward me. I caught the bag and Nikolai smiled. "Bring me back that bastard's corpse. I have uses for him."

~7~

Belle was quiet in the truck for about half the trip to the group home: a pretty bizarre state for her, really, and one that had me a little worried. When she finally did speak, though, it did nothing to ease things.

"I'm sorry, Mac. I didn't mean to make you angry. I just thought..."

"I'm not angry, Belle." She still scowled when I interrupted her. "I'm not. I'm just... I'm worried about what we're heading into."

"That's why I asked Coralia for the mask." She sounded so defeated. Sad. It was killing me. "I thought it would be better if I..."

"Damn it, Belle..." I veered into a mini-mart lot and slammed the truck in park. With the truck stopped, I turned in my seat and looked at her. "I know you did this for me and... it was probably the right call... but you gotta understand... I have lost almost everything in my life and the one thing I could always count on *not* losing was you." I sucked in a deep breath. "Taking you into this shit is not... Belle, I'm scared."

"Mac..." She set her hand on my thigh. I'm sure it was supposed to be comforting or something, but it really didn't help my state of mind. "I'm scared, too. That's why I insisted on coming with you. I thought if I was a woman, it would be easier f..."

"And you are a woman." She scowled again and it was so damned adorable. Fuck. I squeezed my eyes shut and shook my head. "You are an incredibly beautiful fucking woman, Belle, and do you know what happens to beautiful women around me?! They end up dead!" I punched the dash and she jumped a little in her seat. "Dead, Belle! Every time!" I was losing it. "And I can't... I can't..."

"Alex..." Her voice was quiet. Soft. Hypnotic. "Look at me."

I took a deep breath and turned toward her, forcing my eyes to stay focused on her face.

"We will deal with the cauchemar then we will go home." She reached over and wrapped her hand around my fingertips. "Together. Okay?"

I felt myself nodding. "Okay." I checked the mirror and put the truck back in drive. "Okay. Let's do this."

The rest of the trip to the home was a little better. She wasn't her normal chattering self, but she wasn't sitting in the passenger seat in total silence either. She reminded me of details: the few weaknesses cauchemar possess, the ways this one was behaving differently, and how much power it took to be able to control a creature like that.

She was amazing. Captivating in every sense. Every bit the definition of magical, which made sense considering she actually was a magical creature currently walking around in a human skin. I kept stealing glances: her body, her face, the way the sunlight danced in her eyes and...

"Is the *domovoi* messing with your head, Mac?"

"I don't think so." What the hell kind of question was that? "Why?"

"You're acting different." She sounded concerned and I knew I needed to say something to ease her mind, but I was having a hard time coming up with anything that didn't sound insane. "I just want to make sure you're okay."

"I'm fine, Belle." Yeah, I lied. I wasn't fine but my *domovoi* co-pilot had nothing to do with it.

There wasn't much of the trip left and we spent it in silence: Belle going through the purse of charms Nikolai had packed for her and me lost in dozens of thoughts I really didn't need to be having. At least when she quit talking directly to me, I didn't automatically glance over at her every time I heard her voice.

"Shit." I pulled up across the street from the group home, carefully identifying the various emergency vehicles on the scene.

"What's wrong, Mac?"

Just as Belle asked what was wrong, I found what I was looking for: the coroner's van.

"Someone's dead, Belle." I looked over at her just in time to see her eyes fill with tears and wanted to kick myself. I knew how deeply she felt things and, particularly knowing what we were going into, I should have been more sensitive to how she would react. To me, whoever was in the body bag being wheeled out the house was just a glitch in the job... but she wasn't me. I laid my arm across the back of the seat. "C'mere."

She slid across the seat and laid her head against my chest, weeping almost immediately. "I'm sorry, Belle." I wrapped my arms around her and kissed the top of her head. "I forget that we don't see things the same way."

"You are *sang pejuang*." I had no idea what she just called me or how I was supposed to respond, so I didn't. "You don't have the freedom to be bothered by it. That's why it's so terrible when it's close to you."

Here I thought it was just that I was an asshole that didn't give a shit but I was floating in a completely inexplicable state of knowing exactly what she meant and not understanding her at all; all compounded by me hating myself for all the things that were teasing the back of my brain as I sat there with her in my arms. And there was nothing to do but wait.

"Let's get out of here." She needed a break from the emotional trauma, and I needed to be someplace other than trapped in the cab of the truck with her. "Go get a coffee while they finish up, huh?"

The sound of my voice registered in my brain about the time she looked up at me and smiled.

"I haven't heard that accent in a long time, Mac." She slid back into the passenger seat and pulled on her seatbelt. "I kinda missed it, to be honest."

I snapped my seatbelt back on, cursed under my breath, and started the truck. *That accent* was my mother's creole blood pouring out of my mouth: something I'd worked hard to bury as a young teen and had almost completely forgotten until it came out just now. But I *really* didn't need the woman sitting next to me to be so intrigued by its sudden return.

I drove to a coffee shop I'd seen on my trip to the group home the day before and we went inside. It was a quiet, cozy, intimate sort of place that made me wish I'd spied one of those busy every-other-corner chain places instead. Of course, Belle thought it was the perfect place to wait out the activity at the group home. She asked me what I wanted and I just shook my head. I wasn't in the mindset to pick out some fancy coffee and the only thing I really wanted right now definitely wasn't on their menu board. I handed her my wallet, told her to surprise me, and walked toward the *restroom* sign at the back of the cafe.

A couple handfuls of cold water to the face and a stern conversation with the asshole in the mirror later, I walked back out into the dining room and sat at the little table across from Belle. The table she'd picked and the seat she'd left open settled me with my back in a corner and a clear view of both entrances: basically the perfect location. I wasn't surprised.

I lost track of how long we sat there, trying to look like the cute normal couple the other customers saw sitting there. When the string of emergency vehicles started to pass by the window I nodded slowly.

"Finish your drink, Belle. It's showtime."

The group home administrator was on the porch when I parked.

"I thought I saw your truck earlier." She was smiling. Flirty. Christ, how long did that damned charm last? "But things were a little crazy around here."

"I noticed. What happened?"

Her smile broke but I wasn't sure if it was my question or the fact that Belle got out of the truck.

"Kelly Randall died last night."

The cauchemar's first victim. What was the connection? "What happened?"

"They have to do an autopsy." She suddenly sounded weak. Scared. "Her chest was all bruised but there was…" She shook her head. I knew the look. She was trying to make sense of something that she didn't understand. Couldn't understand. "The look on her face…"

"Okay." I set my hand on her shoulder, hoping it would be some sort of soothing. "We need to see her room again."

She nodded, gave Belle a look I didn't even want to try to translate, and led us inside.

Halfway up the stairs, Belle grabbed my hand. I looked back over my shoulder, completely unprepared for the terror on her face. "It's here, Mac."

I didn't know if she meant the cauchemar or whatever was controlling it, but it didn't really matter. If it had her that scared, I needed to stay sharp.

The administrator showed us to Kelly's room and glared at Belle before I shut the door.

"Well, *she's* charming." At least Critter hadn't lost her sense of humor behind that damned mask.

"Charmed, actually." Belle glared at me. "What? She wasn't going to give me any information yesterday. No access to the place at all." I knew why I was explaining myself but that didn't make it any better.

"It's okay, Mac. I really don't care about her, I just…"

Her eyes were locked on something behind me. Had I really been that stupid? "Belle?"

She nodded as she reached into her purse. "I think she'll be disappointed when she finds out about us, is all." I let my hand move to the hilt of the Ubojica. She nodded again.

I took a step toward her, slowly drawing the enchanted blade. I could smell it behind me, now: ashes, sulfur, the stench of rotting flesh. I couldn't remember if those were the tells for a cauchemar or not but the only reason it mattered was to make sure I aimed for the right spot. Whatever it was, it was there. Belle and I were going to have to face it. Now.

Cauchemar tend to appear as hideously deformed humanoids with large patches of rotting flesh. For the most part, they climb on the chests of their victims, crush them and – assuming the poor sap doesn't die of fright first – devour their lifeforce. From the administrator's description, Kelly Randall could have gone either way and, now, her murderer was behind me and I was the only thing between it and one of the few things in the universe that actually mattered to me. When all was said and done, all that boiled down to a single fact: it was between me and the cauchemar and only one of us was leaving this room alive.

Belle pulled her hand from her purse wearing a couple rings she hadn't been wearing before. I wasn't sure what they were, but it wasn't the time to ask.

Nan montre tan.

Showtime.

I spun on my heel with the Ubojica held about neck level. The cauchemar and I were roughly the same height. That made things a little more interesting but it wasn't enough to give it the upper hand. It ducked back as I spun, just barely avoiding the tip of the blade. The cauchemar hissed and lunged at me, apparently expecting its appearance to shock or stagger me in some way. It was too far into its attack when it realized I hadn't even flinched: it couldn't stop and I wasn't about to let the superhuman force of its attack go to waste.

It saw me move and threw its weight to the side: the move that should have buried the Ubojica in its gut ended with the blade taking a thick slice from its shoulder but that wasn't enough to stop it. It wasn't even enough to really slow it down. It shouldn't have been able to adjust like that: either its puppeteer was close by or I really was getting too old for this.

Almost as if it was responding to my own self-doubt, I felt the *domovoi's* power rush through me: filling me with a strength and speed I wasn't completely sure I was going to be able to use. It overwhelmed my senses. My body moved on its own and the Ubojica glinted in the sunlight just as my fist buried it in the side of the cauchemar's neck.

The monster howled. Or maybe it was me. Or maybe I was a monster. The cauchemar fell and I followed it to the floor, driving another knife through its shoulder. Another through its arm. I had lost control: the bloodlust of the *domovoi* had taken over and I wasn't going to be content until I'd torn the damned thing apart, preferably with my bare hands. I couldn't see anything but the cauchemar's writhing body or hear much of anything over the pounding of my heartbeat in my ears and the grinding of my own teeth.

"Alex McLaren." Her voice cut through the noise. My jaw relaxed and my heartbeat slowed. "Mac?" I flinched when she touched me, but I didn't move away and she didn't move her hand. "Mac, are you with me?"

It hurt to move my jaw. When I tried to nod, I realized it hurt to move at all. "Belle." Even my throat hurt, and my voice was raspy and strained and I could only hope she heard me.

I couldn't really see, yet, but I felt her arms against me: she had her hands on both of my shoulders and I could smell the soft scent of vanilla and cinnamon that drifted off her skin. "Just take it easy, Mac. Don't wrestle for control. Just let the *domovoi* retreat."

I tried to nod but I wasn't sure if my head moved or not. My eyes were starting to focus and I felt a wave of nausea when I looked down at the twitching cauchemar and how far up my arms its black blood had stained my skin.

"Slowly, *cintaku*[4]."

It felt like her voice was the only thing keeping me from tumbling into some black abyss. Fuck you, Nietzsche. The room finally slowed its spinning and the places where Belle was touching me were the only places that weren't in pain. I wanted to bag the cauchemar and get out of there, but I couldn't yet trust my body to do what I wanted it to.

"Easy, Mac." Her voice was so damned soothing: music taming the savage beast.

"Help me." My voice, on the other hand, hit my ears just like the voice of the savage beast. I knew the *domovoi* had to slowly unwind itself from my nervous system but it didn't feel like it was actually letting go and I was losing patience. We needed to get out of there.

"Be patient, Mac." I could focus on her voice and on the warmth of her touch but everything else was still noise and blur and blood. I didn't want to be patient and I didn't want it to go slow... I wanted to be in control of my own body before I completely lost my mind.

"Belle." My voice was still a growl: deep and cold. The sound of her name in that voice disgusted me: an obscene mockery of everything that I was. "You have to leave."

"No." There was no hesitation. No question in her response. "I'm not leaving you, Mac."

---

[4] My love

"I'm not me, *cheri*." I wanted to sigh but I growled instead, and her touch fluttered slightly. She flinched. I wanted to scream but I was afraid whatever sound that was would just be worse. "Please, *nanm mwen*.[5] Do as I ask, huh"

Her hands moved but they didn't move away: her body was pressed against my back and her arms wrapped around my chest. The soft vanilla and cinnamon scent was intoxicating and that, at least, was a sensation I could use to my advantage. If there was one way I knew how to function, it was drunk. I felt her skin against the side of my face: felt her kiss my cheek. "*Belahan jiwaku*, you fool. I will never leave you."

I could feel the *domovoi* sinking its claws deeper into my nerves rather than letting go. I had to get her out of there. "Belle, *trezò ki pi valè mwen an*[6], you have to go. I'm losing control of this thing and I can't..." If the *domovoi* harmed one hair on her head, I'd be handing it an express ticket to hell and if it was still in my body when I did... well... I'm supposed to be retired, right?

Her body moved away from mine and I dared to hope she was actually doing as I asked. Those hopes were quickly dashed, of course: her hands returned to my body and a strap of cold circled my neck. Her fingers brushed my skin as she buckled the collar, every faint touch sending sparks through me. She was speaking softly... casting... something that sounded vaguely Russian and more than a little menacing to my ears. (Later, I'd realize it was the hitchhiker that saw the spell as a threat but in that moment, there was no separation between us.)

"What are you doing?"

She kept talking... kept casting... it was driving me nuts. Whatever it was that she was saying, it was causing me physical pain... and she could see it. I could hear it in her voice.

"Belle, stop." I could feel it fighting back against whatever she was doing: digging deeper into my nervous system rather than letting go. Deep in my head I heard it and it occurred to me: whatever it was that was digging its way deeper into my soul *wasn't* the feral benevolent creature I thought it was... whatever it was, it wasn't Nikolai's *domovoi*. Even though he had tricked me into the merger, I couldn't believe Nikolai would lie about what he'd attached to me... which meant this wasn't what he'd prepared Belle to deal with. "You have to leave."

---

[5] My soul

[6] Treasure, precious

She was still there next to me. I could smell her. Vanilla and cinnamon… and desperation. She knew that whatever it was she was doing wasn't working the way it was supposed to, but she wasn't giving up. Damn it. I needed her to give up: to get out of there before I lost my fight with this thing… because I was going to lose. I could feel it.

"Go, Belle."

"NO!" At least she stopped casting… maybe if it wasn't fighting back against the spell, I'd be able to gain some ground. "I won't leave you, Mac!"

"And I love you for it, *nanm mwen*, but you have to!" That was probably going to start a bunch of shit later but right now it didn't matter… I needed her to get out of here before this thing inside me hurt her.

"I have the spells, Mac! I just have to…" She was desperate. Crying. The last time I'd heard that quality in anyone's voice it was my voice begging Stefanie not to die while I wrestled what was left of the car away from her broken body… and knowing how that turned out wasn't doing much for my outlook. "Just let me…"

"Belle." She sobbed when I interrupted her and the sound hit me like a truck. I'd lost my voice almost completely: speaking in the growl of whatever the beast inside me really was. "You have to leave."

"Mac, what's happening?!" She was gasping. Crying. Damn it. "Why isn't it working?!"

I wanted to tell her she had the wrong tools… that the spells she was casting were built to target something else… that the only thing her work was accomplishing was pissing the thing off… but I couldn't gain enough control of my voice to get any of that across. I needed her to get out of the room and I needed it to happen sooner rather than later: I could feel my hold slipping and if she was still here when I lost it there was no telling what would happen. I couldn't see her but I turned my face in the direction of her scent, hoping whatever it was I was fighting would show enough of itself for her to take me seriously. "GO!"

There was a scrambling sound: rushed, frightened. I think she fell backward when I yelled… roared… whatever the hell that sound was. She was scrambling away from me and the only reason I knew it was because it was using all my strength to keep from leaping toward her and ripping her apart. God damn it, Belle, get the fuck out of here! She was still moving away… rushing… there it was.

The creak of the hinges. The crack of the door against the frame.

She was out.

Safe.

Now, I could deal with this thing.

It would have been a hell of a lot easier if I knew what I was dealing with, but I didn't have a lot of choice. If I knew one thing about Belle it was that she wasn't going to go far... and if this thing hurt her...

Why the hell didn't they just let me stay retired?

You're a fool, McLaren.

I talk to myself sometimes, quite a lot actually, but I never call myself 'McLaren' and I don't normally growl at myself... despite the rather unpleasant conversation I had with myself in the restroom mirror at the café earlier.

"Let's cut the shit, shall we?" I don't know if I was actually talking or not... but I was communicating. That was what mattered. "What the fuck are you and what do you want?'

In that order?

"Sure, bitch." Jesus Christ. I end up with a smartass villain too? Assuming whatever the hell I was dealing with actually *was* the villain. "Amuse me."

You're much braver without your lover here. It laughed. It was also getting on my last nerve... but if it thought Belle was my lover, it wasn't as smart as it thought it was. I had a chance. *I always thought it was the other way 'round for your kind.* I just had to figure out how to use its arrogance to my advantage.

"My *kind*? What *kind* is that? Creole? Queer?"

Human.

Oh, come on you son of a bitch. Gimme something I can work with. I already figured you weren't fuckin human.

"What... the fuck... do you want?" It laughed again and I would have clawed my own throat out if I thought it would have made it stop. Whatever was going to happen needed to happen soon: Belle had left, finally, but she wouldn't go far and she wouldn't stay gone long. "Or are you afraid I'm gonna fuck up your plans?"

Afraid? Of you? I could hear it... thankfully. Deep in its attempt at amusement it was afraid... I just needed to know why. *You've quite the high opinion of yourself, soldier.*

"Yeah, well..." Come on, you bastard! "I got a gorgeous girl that thinks I'm pretty great. What do you have?"

At the moment, McLaren, I have you.

"Quit talking in circles, dick." Yanking the Ubojica from the cauchemar's corpse and cutting this asshole out of me was getting more and more appealing. "What do you want."

I wanted you to know that you cannot win. Not this time.

"Is that it?" I could feel it actually letting go, but I wasn't ready to trust it. Not yet. Not until it was fully gone. "All this just to prove your supposed superiority? Damn, have you got a fuckin complex."

See you soon.

I wanted to answer with some snarky 'can't wait' or something, but the asshole wouldn't even let me get the last word: it tore itself out of my system in a single move, leaving every nerve raw and every synapse momentarily fried. My brain recovered quickly enough but my body wasn't as quick to bounce back. I was vaguely aware of the fact that I was on the floor and making some sort of noise... moaning, crying, screaming, maybe all of the above. The pain was enough to make me almost wish the fucker hadn't left at all... no. That wasn't accurate. It really needed to be gone... I just wish it hadn't felt the need to take the cheap shot on its way out.

It occurred to me as I lay there in excruciating pain that I didn't know how much of the manticore's natural abilities Belle retained while she was masked. At this point, I was really only concerned with one of her many superhuman traits: her incredibly acute hearing. Whatever that thing was, it had done some serious damage and I wasn't entirely sure I should move... assuming I even could. My throat felt dry but slick with blood at the same time and I wasn't sure how much noise I could actually make but I had to try... unless I was just going to lay there until someone decided to check on the room. "It's gone." Even trying to speak sent searing pain through my entire body. I was paralyzed. And it felt like I was bleeding. "I need you."

~8~

There was something different about the house, but I couldn't put my finger on it... something just felt different. I walked through the living room to the kitchen and, while I would have given just about anything for this to be right, I knew immediately what was wrong.

"Mac, baby." Stefanie set the pan back on the stove and walked across the kitchen toward me. "You're home early."

I felt myself nodding but I was too stunned to speak. What the hell was going on? Stefanie stopped and tilted her head to the side like she did when she was trying to figure something out.

"Baby?" She looked so damned concerned. "Is everything okay?"

"I... um..."

She reached out and grabbed my hands the way she always used to... stepping close and stretching to up kiss me. "What's wrong?"

"I... uh..." You're dead, baby. That's what's wrong. "Um..."

Off to the left, I heard a clock chime. My grandmother's clock. The one that hung in the kitchen of her Spring Valley home when I was a child.

The home that had been destroyed by a fire almost twenty years ago.

Stefanie's head snapped toward the clock.

"You really *are* early, baby." Now she really sounded worried. "You... you shouldn't be here."

"Wha..?"

She pulled away from me, pacing the kitchen floor and wringing her hands like she always did when she was waiting for something important to happen. "You're not supposed to be here, yet, Mac. They're not done with you."

"Who's..? Wha..?" I shook my head. She wasn't making any sense and, honestly, I didn't even want to know what was happening. I was with Stefanie again... that was all I cared to know.

"You have to leave, Mac." The light in the kitchen was fading. I wanted to argue but I couldn't open my mouth. "It was never your fault, baby. Forgive yourself." She kissed me softly as the room grew dark. "I'll see you when it's time."

"Damn it, Mac, wake up!" It took a minute for Belle's voice to register in my brain but, even when it did, I still couldn't respond.

"Do not worry, little one." I didn't want to be relieved at the sound of Nikolai's voice right now, but I was. I kinda wanted to reach out and choke the shit out of him but I couldn't force myself to do that either.

I couldn't make myself do anything: not move, not speak, nothing. It was like I was... oh shit. I was dead. That's where I was... in the kitchen with Stef... I was dead and apparently, I still was. Mostly, at least.

"Alex, please!" Belle sounded like she was losing her mind. Again. I knew the pain in her voice all too well and I hated the fact that I was the reason for it.

Stef said I had to go and Belle wanted me here... why the hell was I stuck in this hellish limbo where I couldn't reach either of them? Was this normal? Had whatever that thing was put some sort of curse on me? Being dead was about the only thing I could think of I didn't have any experience with and that annoying little tidbit of information was driving me crazy.

"Come away, child." Coralia's voice. She must have been talking to Belle. "Let Nikolai see if he can discover what is keeping our Alex from returning to us, no?" Belle whimpered something that sounded vaguely like she'd agreed and then Coralia's voice again: hushed and anxious. "Find *something*, Nikolai."

More shuffling sounds. A door closing softly. Nikolai muttering something in Russian that I couldn't quite hear and probably wouldn't have understood if I could. A faint scent hit my nose, slowly growing stronger: a warm woodsy medicine sort of smell. I was pretty sure I'd smelled it before... some sort of incense... but I couldn't tell you what kind.

Shit... I couldn't tell you anything right now, but that's beside the point.

"Oh, *otprysk*, what did I do wrong?"

God, Nik, don't use this time to second-guess yourself. Come on, man! What if this limbo shit has a timer and it ends up permanent if you don't fix it?

"I do not see any sense of permanency to this." I could sense, more than anything, the way Nikolai was circling the table. "Like this is some sort of sick joke. Meant for what, though?"

Ask the asshole you helped hitch a ride in my soul, Nik. Come *on!* Figure this out before it *really* becomes a problem.

"And what was it that decided to take the place of the *domovoi?* What has the power?"

If I fuckin knew that, I wouldn't be lying here *dead!* I'd have known how to fight the bastard.

"You could not possibly have been prepared for this, Alex."

What the hell? Is he actually answering me?

"Whatever it was that managed to do this is far beyond any of the weapons I sent with you."

Well, that's fuckin comforting. I could hear Nikolai muttering again but I couldn't tell if he was actually doing anything or just grumbling. Whatever it was that he was doing, the sound of it was dark and defeated... grim even for the Russian's standards. Come on, Nik. If anyone can figure this shit out, it's you.

He was still circling me, still trying to verbally work through what had happened. Trying to figure out what went wrong. He stopped walking and set his hand on my shoulder which wouldn't have been such a phenomenal action to me except that I felt it. I could feel his hand on my shoulder. Come on, Nik! I'm here.

"You're in there somewhere, aren't you? I can feel it." He patted my shoulder. I think he was trying to be reassuring, but I'm not sure if he really believed I could process it or if it was just to make himself feel better. "You have to say goodbye to Stefania, *otprysk.* She knows this and so do you." He *did* know what was going on... better than I did, apparently. "You will return to her when the time is right. Now, we need you here and she knows this as well as you do."

Could it really be that simple? I never really considered myself as having a death wish but, lying here dead, I was kinda beginning to see the signs. It had been five years since Stefanie died and, in that time, the only things I'd really been able to do were drink more and care less. Critter got me out of bed in the morning and spending time with Sammy forced me into the world but, without them, I probably would have been face-down in a ditch somewhere long ago.

And that last moment before she disappeared... that last kiss... Stefanie told me to forgive myself. I'd never been able to deny her anything and, as much as I may have wanted to continue beating myself up for the rest of my life, if I didn't wake up and get up off the damned table I wasn't going to have any more time to even try to come to terms with the accident that killed Stefanie and just how responsible for it I may or may not have been.

"Did you just move?"

I don't know, Nik. Did I? He lifted my left hand and I felt his hands close around mine.

"You need to come back, now, *otprysk*. The ladies are worried sick."

I wanted to laugh at the thought of Coralia and Belle being worried about me, but I'd heard them. And I knew better than to laugh *at* either of them... but Nikolai using them as the reason I had to wake up. That was still kind of funny. I wanted to laugh. I actually tried to laugh. It didn't quite work out the way I'd hoped it would, though.

It was less laughing and more gasping and choking: extreme discomfort rather than amusement.

But it happened. That was the important part.

Nikolai slipped his arm behind my shoulder and helped me sit up. I was struggling to fill my lungs: it was like my body had forgotten what it was supposed to do. It didn't take much for it to remember, though. A moment later I was sucking huge amounts of air into my lungs, sweating bullets, and shaking like my mother-in-law's thanksgiving jello mold. My vision was starting to clear: my body starting to register something besides pain and numbness.

"Nik?"

"Alex! *Slava Bogu!*" For the first time in the twenty-five years (give or take) that I'd known him, I saw tears in Nikolai's eyes. "I thought we lost you!"

"I think you did for a bit, there." I could see the workshop clearly now and, honestly, it made sense that's where I was. Critter couldn't exactly have taken me to the hospital: though the pain and weakness that filled my body when I tried to move made me wonder if maybe she should have anyway.

"Slowly!" Nik was beside me, helping me to my feet since he'd realized I was determined not to stay on the worktable any longer. "Easy, you stubborn ass! You're mortally wounded, you know."

"I'm getting better."

His laughter was weak and forced, but it was good to hear.

My intention had been to walk to the door, but it ended up being more a shuffling attempt not to fall that was only successful thanks to a hell of a lot of support from Nikolai.

"You are a damned fool, Alex. You need rest." And yet, he was still helping me walk.

What I needed was proof that I actually *was* alive and just being in Nik's workshop, no matter how emotional he seemed at my recovery, wasn't quite doing it.

Once I was in the hall, I had a little more control of my movement. I was getting stronger, slowly, but now I could use the wall to keep me upright as I headed toward the kitchen. I could hear Belle crying and Coralia trying to soothe her and, in that moment, that was the only thing that mattered. I reached the entry and leaned against the wall. Belle was still wearing her human mask, weeping on Coralia's shoulder.

"You know, I hate to see a pretty girl cry." She turned toward me and relief smoothed the pain and worry from her face. "Is there anything I can do to help?"

"Mac!" One second she was in Coralia's arms and the next she was in mine. If I hadn't already been leaning against the wall, we probably both would've ended up on the floor. Everything about her made me feel more alive in that moment than I had in years: the warmth of her embrace, the smell of vanilla and cinnamon that followed her, the way her body fit so perfectly in my arms. There were easily a hundred reasons I should have been trying to squash the thoughts that were filling my mind but then her lips were on mine. She wasn't timid or hesitant, but the kiss was soft. Gentle.

And, God help me, I was kissing her back.

On the drive home, Belle explained she'd chosen to keep the mask intact in order to better care for me after the incident: citing the benefits of normal height, opposable thumbs, and the ability to answer the door and phone if necessary, and the realization that she actually liked driving my truck. I tried to laugh at that one, but it hurt too much. She didn't say she was worried that I might not pull through or that she feared I'd be useless even if I did, but she didn't have to. I could hear it in her voice.

"Come on, Belle." I'd given up trying to silence my accent. At least for the time being. I was still running on very limited resources and sounding like last century's river pirate wasn't going to make or break anything in the grand scheme of things. "You know it'll take more than some *kidnape avyon mons*[7] for you to get rid of me."

She glared at me from the seat beside me but didn't say anything. I don't know what she was thinking but whatever it was she wasn't going to share it with me. Not right now, anyway. We drove the rest of the way in silence but I

---

[7] Monster hijacker

knew it wasn't going to last. I also knew that I really didn't know what to do next. She wasn't Belle, after all. She was Critter. And regardless of all the things that went through my mind when I looked at her, I had to remember that. And she *was* Belle. Damn it.

The fact that she kept her mask on in order to take care of me was probably a good thing, though.

See: when I thought I was broken... laying there bleeding... I was. A lot. The thing – whatever it was – had ripped its way out of me: leaving not only the frayed ends of my nervous system to deal with, but a jagged gaping hole in the side of my chest as well. So the fall, and the bleeding, and the excruciating pain and debilitating weakness were all real.

Awesome.

And we were still no closer to finding out what it was that had taken the *domovoi*'s place. No closer to finding out anything about what it was, why it had used a cauchemar to terrorize a rehab group home, or why it felt the need to prove to me that I couldn't beat it.

I needed answers.

I needed to know what I was fighting, and I needed to know how to beat it.

"You're not fighting anything right now, Mac," Belle said softly as she traced runes on the side of my chest around the wound. "And you need time to…"

"I need to kill that son of a bitch."

I hadn't been prepared for the snarl that replaced my voice and, judging from the way she pulled her hand away, neither had Belle.

"Mac?" Her voice was shaky: timid. "Are you okay?"

I ground my teeth to keep them together and closed my eyes. I just had to sound halfway normal. "I'm fine, Belle." I don't think I managed it but she resumed her runework, so I have to assume she went ahead and accepted my lie. She damned sure wasn't dumb enough to actually believe it.

~10~

Of all the looks I've been forced to wear throughout my life, helpless and weak definitely weren't ones that got a lot a mileage. In fact, the number of times I'd actually consciously succumbed to either could be counted on one hand with fingers left over. Avoiding those states was, according to the theories of people who were dumb enough to give a shit about me, one of the reasons I drink like I do.

Whatever.

The only reason that particular bit of information matters in the least is that it explains why I, like the idiot I'm assured I am, refused to stay in bed and be waited on and tended to like a fucking invalid. I was sitting on the edge of the bed, trying to keep my head from spinning, when Belle came into the room.

"You should be lying down."

"I should fucking be doing something about this."

Her voice had been soft. Kind. There was less than zero reason for me to snap at her.

"Like what?"

It was a simple question: one I should know the answer to... but all I could do was snarl in response.

"Mac?" Soft. Caring. "You okay?" Why was it pissing me off?

"I'm fine."

She sat next to me on the edge of the bed and set her hand on my shoulder. It should have been comforting. Soothing. Rather than let it affect me, though, I shrugged violently and growled.

"Yeah. You sound fine."

"What the hell do you want me to say, Belle?" I finally looked up and immediately wished I hadn't. The room wasn't really spinning any more, which was a good thing, but Belle... she looked like she wanted to either run from the room or start crying. "I have a scar the size of Rhode Island where some otherworlder literally blew out my side and we're no closer to having any idea why."

She shrunk away as I ranted. That, finally, was enough to make me feel something other than frustration and anger.

"Fuck, Belle, I'm sorry. I..."

"Ssh." She smiled weakly and slowly set her hand on my knee. "Don't, Mac. It's okay."

It wasn't okay and we both knew it, but I couldn't bring myself to argue with her. All through my recovery, which felt like it was taking forever due to the combination of magical and physical damage the bastard had done to me, I'd become an even bigger asshole than usual: snapping at her for pretty much no reason, growling when I should just be talking... it was like that darkness that had taken over when I was fighting the cauchemar had left some bit of itself behind.

Even though I was mostly healed, physically at any rate, she refused to take off the mask. It didn't take long to realize that she actually liked being Belle. The only problem was that I liked her being Belle, too. A lot. Too much.

I never felt lonely after Stef died because I was never alone. She had always been here: sharing my thoughts, my dreams, my fears. Keeping me sane. The only difference, now, was that she was actually a woman and able to do more to take care of me than she'd ever been able to do before. As much as I wanted to believe I didn't need to be taken care of, I knew better... I had always known better... and she'd always been the one to take care of me.

All that's to explain why, like a damned idiot, I didn't tell her to get out of my bed that first night she curled up against me. Don't get me wrong. It wasn't bad. It wasn't bad at all, if you catch my drift. But it did make things a hell of a lot more complicated.

The weird part was that nothing had really changed but, at the same time, it was like everything had. It never occurred to me that I might have felt lonely after Stef died: I was never alone, after all. But there was a powerful difference between having Critter flitting around the house and having Belle in my arms.

I'd been trying not to think too much about all the implications of what was happening but when Sammy told me it was okay that I had a new girlfriend and that he really liked her... well... that pretty much removed my ability to ignore the facts. And it could have been worse, I suppose: at least I fell for someone who knew what she was getting into.

Even if she was a manticore.

Yeah... my life's a little fucked up.

Nik, of course, has been giving me a ton of shit about. It's not like he's really got any room to talk: he's married to a fuckin mermaid, for God's sake.

The biggest problem for me was that, the better I felt, the more I wanted to go after the bastard that did this to me and neither Belle nor I could figure out what it was or why it did it. Of course, honestly, I didn't really care much about the details: I just wanted to kick its ass.

Nik couldn't come up with anything either, which was even more frustrating.

Every clue we found was just another dead end.

Of course, I'd been a dead end a few weeks back so there's that.

The weather was starting to change, though, and the cold was starting to sink into everyone's bones. Halloween was just around the corner: the perfect time for this shit.

I had to be ready and I had to be on my guard.

~11~

You know that feeling when things are too perfect and everything's about to go to shit? When you're just sure of it? Yeah, I was there. It was like my life had been a dream since I'd died. Even Stef hadn't made me feel the way I felt with Belle and the relatively quiet life we'd been leading was good.

So good.

Even my assholish tendencies and more frequent than normal outbursts hadn't done any real damage to the general tranquility.

So, of course, it all had to go to hell. It always did.

The last time I'd felt this good, Stef died.

That was all I needed to justify my decision and why I was where I was right now: driving across the county in the middle of the night in response to the only call I'd ever actually hidden from Belle. It was a lead, though - the first real one we'd had - and all I could do was hope she'd forgive me if I lived through this and managed to come home to her.

When I pulled up the address I'd been given there was no doubt I was in the right place.

The house looked like the set of a no-budget horror film. You know the ones that when, after you watch it, you can't decide if it was supposed to really be a monster flick or just a dire warning about the dangers of inbreeding.

This was the place, though.

I could feel it.

It was here.

It was going after the kind of people that didn't call for help. It would have been a fluke that I'd heard about it at all unless it had orchestrated the whole thing. The fact that it had intentionally drawn me out into the middle of nowhere with no hope of back-up didn't really occur to me until I was climbing out of the truck.

Alone.

Like a fuckin idiot.

You know, at some point, you think I'd learn.

Maybe I'd make it out of this alive. Or Nik will be able to bring me back again. Either way, Belle was gonna be pissed.

But I could feel it here. Taunting me.

I had to take care of this damned thing once and for all.

The guy walking out of the house didn't do much to change my opinion of the place or my current situation. He moved like he was in his twenties but looked about seventy: craggy and grizzled and seriously not in the mood to deal with any bullshit.

I knew the feeling.

"You the one called about the thing?"

In a normal situation, I probably would have been annoyed at having to decipher whatever the hell it was the guy had just said. Tonight, though: in this space and with all that was happening, it kinda just made perfect sense. "That's right."

He looked me up and down. Suspicious. It may have just been his nature but it may have been him doubting my abilities, it was hard to tell. And the grunt he gave me in response didn't really give me much of a clue. He twitched his head toward the house before turning away from me. "C'mon then."

It was all the invitation I was going to get so I followed him up the half-built (or half-demolished, it was hard to say) stairs and across the porch, careful to avoid the places darkened by rot and the stains of God-knows-what.

The inside of the house wasn't much better than the outside: garbage of indeterminate age and origin was a foot or more deep in most of the rooms I could see. The place was cold in spots, warm in others, and generally uncomfortable and more than a little disturbing. In fact, if I couldn't actually *feel* the damned thing here, taunting me, I probably would have written off the kid's condition as whatever passes for natural causes in a place like this.

The man was leading me deeper into the house: past a couple doors closed against some fairly disturbing sounds. "He's back here." The longer I was stuck in this house, the more likely I was going to be to just burn it and salt the earth without a hell of a lot of care about what or who did or didn't get out. In a tiny back room, that may actually have been a walk-in closet at some point in its existence, a young man lay curled up on a ratty uncovered mattress. It was hard to tell much about him: other than the fact that he was either in pain or terrified. Or both. "Dunno what you think you can do for him," the older man scoffed. "But someone gotta do somethin."

"Can we have some privacy?"

The man scowled then shrugged. "Whatever." He backed out of the room, shaking his head, and pulled the door closed behind him.

I waded through the garbage on the floor and stood beside the bed. Now that I was closer and could see his features a little better, I guessed the boy was somewhere around ten or eleven. Right about Sammy's age. That bastard thought of everything.

"You okay, bud?" The kid didn't move: just lay there curled up. Whimpering. Maybe crying. It was hard to tell and, for all the stupid decisions I'd made tonight, getting too close to someone that might be possessed by the bastard I was hunting wasn't gonna be one. "Kid?"

The boy finally stirred. He didn't really acknowledge my existence so much as just recognize that there was someone else there. It was a start.

"You alright?"

I could barely hear him: his voice was weak and faint but it was there. "It hurts."

Now, at least, we might be getting somewhere. "What hurts?"

"Everything."

Damn, kid. Gimme something to work with here. "What happened?"

The boy slowly unfolded his body, rolling over so he could face me... if you could call it facing me considering the state of the kid's face, that is. The last time I'd seen someone's face that messed up, I was looking in a mirror after a particularly bloody knock-down with a troll and the time before that, I was having a few choice words with the drunk driver that had been speeding the wrong way up a dark road and killed my wife.

"I din do nothin wrong." The kid was on the defensive. Scared. Jesus Christ, what was wrong with these people?

"I know that." The kid reminded me so much of Sammy that just seeing him like this was making me nauseous. I didn't even want to think about what had actually happened to the poor kid. "Just tell me what happened." I said I didn't want to think about it... that doesn't mean I had that luxury.

"I was workin outside." I felt like a dick: standing there with my arms crossed over my chest instead of doing something - *anything* - to comfort the poor kid. "An a man come up an said he need my help. So Imma go help him."

"Alright."

"I go wit him to by his car and he turns a right monster." The poor kid was terrified just talking about it. "I ain't lyin!"

"I know." God, I needed a drink. This poor kid. Shit, *he* probably needed a drink. "What did he look like? When he turned into the monster?"

"Lots t'like he looked before except more scary in his eyes."

Not terribly helpful but not entirely useless. "What about his eyes?"

"They went all black an empty... like there wasn't nothin there. Nothin but a black fire."

That narrowed it a little but not enough for me to really get a handle on what I was facing. "Then what?"

"He started talkin weird. Sayin things I don't understand. Some diff'ernt kinda talkin."

"Saying weird things or like a whole other language?"

"It was a whole nother language."

"Can you remember *anything* he said?" It was a shot in the dark, but it was the best one I had. If the kid could remember anything at all, I might be able to figure out who I was dealing with... or, at the very least, what kind of shape the poor kid really was in.

"I... um..." He was trying. I could see it. But I also knew before he slumped and sighed and started apologizing that he wasn't going to come up with anything. That would've been too much like giving me a break.

"It's okay, bud." It wasn't, really... but he needed to think it was. With no idea what the mysterious man was saying, or even what language he was saying it in, I was right back where I started. "Do you believe in magic?"

The kid looked shocked by the question and, honestly, a little worried. "Pa says there ain't no such a thing."

Figures. "Well, I didn't ask what Pa says."

Even though he was in pain and scared half out of his mind, the boy smiled a little and nodded.

"Good." I fished one of Nikolai's trinkets out of my jacket pocket: a small metal figure of a knight. It looked like it had been painted before, but the details had been worn away by time. What it looked like wasn't really the issue, though. I held it out to the boy and waited until he closed his hand around it. "That's a paladin." Blank stare. No clue. Okay. "It's like a knight but kinda stronger because it's got God on its side."

"Really?"

"Really." As long as the layered charms actually kick in when they're supposed to, at any rate. "So, it'll protect you, but it'll also help you feel better."

The boy tightened his hold on the figure. It was hard to tell in the room's weak light but it looked like some of the bruising was already beginning to fade. "Are you a paladin too?"

I laughed but managed not to answer with the first thing that came to mind. See, I'd been called a lot of things since my life took this fucked up turn into the unknown but paladin had never been one of them. "Nah. I'm just a knight with a bad attitude."

And jack shit to go on.

"You gonna be okay, kid?"

The boy nodded. In his defense, I don't think he knew he was lying... and I didn't have the nerve to tell him. Whatever the thing was that had attacked him had branded him: I saw it on the inside of the boy's wrist when I handed him the trinket. The only way I could guarantee this kid would, in fact, be okay was if I killed the thing that attacked him. The one that killed me. The one I still couldn't even identify.

I left the house feeling defeated. The only thing I'd accomplished was helping the kid be a little more comfortable while he waited for his doom.

The guy that had been walking up the sidewalk stopped next to my truck. "That's not the only thing you accomplished, McLaren."

That voice. No fuckin way. "Do I know you?"

"Don't you recognize me?" The man smiled and spread his arms as if we might embrace. That wasn't happening and we both knew it, but he seemed determined to appear friendly or something.

"Yeah, well, you look a little different when you're not hijacking my nervous system."

He took a step toward me, still smiling, and it took every spec of discipline I'd ever possessed not to sock him right in his jaw as he approached me. I really wanted to, and I was sure he certainly deserved it, but this guy had killed me when he decided to blow out the side of my chest. I wasn't really looking for a repeat performance of that one. "What do you think is gonna happen here?"

"A friendly conversation." Are you fuckin kidding me? "Nothing more."

"And you had to damn near kill a kid to have a friendly conversation?!"

"I had to get your attention somehow." He shrugged. Now, I really wanted to hit him. "And this seemed the most efficient method."

My fists were clenching: my teeth grinding. "What... the fuck... do you want?"

"I want you to retire, McLaren."

I took a step to the side and leaned against the bed of the truck to keep myself from falling over. I was laughing too hard to stand up unassisted, let alone respond.

"I'm sure my motives are clear enough. I don't…"

"You… ah… you don't understand…" I was trying like hell to stop laughing long enough to have an actual conversation but the best I could do was rushing through the highlights as I laughed. "I've been trying… for twenty-five fuckin years… to get them to quit calling…"

You know that look people get when they can't believe they just heard what was said: that it was just so damned ludicrous that there was no possible way it could be true? Seeing that look on the face your mind has already identified as pure unadulterated evil… fucking hilarious!

"Wait… what?"

I took a couple deep gasping breaths to steady myself, nodding the whole time. "Seriously. Look at me, man. Do I *look* like I want to be out here hunting monsters?" He still looked completely confused so I patted my beat up, dented up, chipped paint truck. "My truck is older now than I was when I started this shit. I'm tired, man."

"I… I don't understand…"

"This is a game for the young, man. Dealing with assholes like you?" I finally stopped laughing enough to speak clearly. "Humans have got expiration dates and I am *way* too old for this shit."

"But you're here." He really was not processing what I was saying.

"Yeah, that's in the fine print." There was a voice in my head telling me that I shouldn't be giving this creature too much information but that same voice was quick to concede that I, technically, wasn't *the* chosen and hadn't been for a very long time. "I didn't die young, so now I'm stuck being punished for it. It's a lifetime appointment. It actually causes physical pain if you ignore the call."

"That's barbaric."

"Says the guy that tortured a kid to get my attention?!"

"Which should give you a little perspective on just how barbaric it really is."

The problem, of course, was that he was right. While the overseers' ability to inflict pain on those that had been sucked into this war had been something many had questioned over the years, it really took having this creep stand here and call it *barbaric* for me to see just how fucked up the whole situation truly was.

He lifted one open hand, palm facing me. The mark I'd seen on the kid's wrist slowly burned into his hand then faded.

"I've released the child." Now it was my turn to be completely confused. "You are a formidable opponent, McLaren. One I'd rather not engage unless it's absolutely necessary."

"Where does that leave this, then?"

He shrugged. "I'll try to stay off your radar."

"There's just one problem with that." See… no matter how formidable I might be or if that was the reason the overseers kept pulling me off the bench when I should have been erased from their pages long ago, there was one thing I just couldn't let go of with this guy. "You killed me."

"And you recovered."

"Right. Because that's what the fuckin hero types do."

He chuckled and shook his head. "No, McLaren. It's *not* what heroes do." He shrugged and took a few steps toward me. "In fact, it's not what *people* do at all."

I really wasn't sure I wanted to hear what came next, but still… "What the hell are you talking about?"

He shrugged and vanished: fading into the night like the last notes of a nightmare anthem I never wanted to hear again.

Not what people do at all… what the hell kind of shit was that?

~12~

There were lights on inside the house when I pulled into the driveway. Belle had woken up and found me gone. Christ, this was gonna be fun. I pulled into the garage and hit the button clipped to the visor to close the door behind me. Once I shut the truck off, I sat there, parked in the dark garage, longer than I probably should have. I couldn't get his parting words out of my head and, if I was honest about it, I didn't want to face Belle's anger either. Not yet. Not while I was still trying to process the accusation that I might be something other than human. I felt a sick laugh in my throat: I was sitting here worried about not being human because my manticore girlfriend was going to be pissed that I took off to fight evil without her. Yeah… that made fuckin loads of sense.

I climbed out of the truck and walked toward the door that led into the kitchen.

Belle was sitting on the counter: her hair was pulled over to one side, her shoulders pressed back against the cabinets, and her bare feet dangling above the floor. There was pretty much no emotion on her face when I walked in and, while I couldn't be sure, I was guessing that wasn't a good thing. At least for me. She reached over and pressed the button on the coffee maker and jumped down off the counter.

The coffee maker popped and hissed as it finished filling the mug. Belle picked up the mug and walked toward me. I was half expecting the steaming coffee to get tossed in my face, but she just put the cup in my hands. "Did you beat it?" She was angry with me… furious… the look on her face and the tone of her voice confirmed it. But there was something else there, too…

Considering the insanity of what had happened tonight, that wasn't as easy to answer as it should have been. I shook my head. The kid was free and it was gone, so any normal person would think I should be nodding right now, yeah? But that last hit…

"Are you hurt?" Her voice was a little higher now. Less controlled. She wanted to stay mad but concern was taking over.

"I..." Again, conventional wisdom and logic said I should say no: that, having taken no physical damage, I should be trying to ease her fears and assure her that everything was fine. "I don't know."

Apparently, that was the tipping point for her. Her arm wrapped around my back and she gently pushed me out of the kitchen and toward the couch in the living room. She took the coffee she'd put in my hands and set it on the table then pushed me back softly. I sat on the couch, watching her as she walked across the room to the bar and came back with a bottle of whiskey in her hand. That part of me that still wasn't sure what exactly was going on expected to either get hit by the bottle or have its contents dumped on my head for some reason, but neither of those things happened. She simply set the bottle on the table next to the coffee cup and sat down beside me.

She pulled her feet up and set her hand on my thigh. "What do you mean you don't know?"

"I went... I was... there was a kid..." Why the hell was it so difficult to explain to her? I'd never had a problem telling her about a battle before. I mean... I guess it hadn't really been a battle tonight so maybe that explained it, but I was pretty sure it had to be a hundred times more complicated than that. "That thing that... that hijacked me... it attacked this kid. Almost destroyed him."

She nodded but didn't say anything. I kinda wish I knew what she was thinking but I was kind of afraid of it, too.

"Beat him to hell. Marked him."

"A kid?"

I nodded and leaned forward, wrapping my hand around the whiskey bottle. I could feel her eyes on me. It was a test. I failed. What else was new?

"A little younger than Sammy." I took a long drink. "Damn near dead when I got there and scared out of his mind." I waited for her to say something. To ask for more details about the kid or start lecturing me about how the booze wasn't going to make the pain go away. Nothing. She was just sitting there, waiting for me to continue. "I got what information I could... gave him a trinket for protection and healing... that's when I saw the mark." The bottle was in my left hand so I lifted it and pointed to the inside of my forearm with my right hand. "There. Deep. Clear as day."

"Were you able to identify it?"

"Never saw it before." I shook my head and took another drink. "But I knew who it belonged to."

"You're sure it was the…"

She couldn't finish her question. Just say it, Belle. The one that killed me. "Yeah. I'm sure."

"But how? If you…"

"Because he was waiting by the truck when I came out of the house."

This time, she didn't scowl when I interrupted her.

"Waiting by the truck?" Her voice was barely louder than a whisper. I'd never heard it that faint before.

I nodded. I could feel bile in my throat as the whole altercation replayed in my head. "Used the kid to get my attention. Shoulda ripped his fuckin head off right then but…" She couldn't say it earlier and, having to see the look on her face if I actually put words to it, I couldn't either. We both knew I was talking about the thing that had killed me: we didn't need verbal reminders. "Said he wants me to retire."

Belle made a sad, sick sound that probably might have been a laugh under less fucked up circumstances.

"Yeah. That was basically my response, too." I took another long drink.

"What else?"

"Huh?" I didn't really think I'd be able to avoid the rest of it, but I'd been hoping.

"With the exception of the details, this all sounds pretty close to normal." As far as I could tell, the only thing relatively normal about it was the fact that I was facing down a monster: but I knew where she was going. What she was after. "There's something more. Something bothering you even more deeply than the boy's similarity to Sam."

I took another drink which, in the grand scheme of things, wasn't going to help my case if I tried to argue with her assessment. And, if I looked at it objectively, I'm not sure it was really as bad as I first thought. I mean… it will have meant that the string of lies I thought I'd been fed throughout my life were actually not the lies that meant anything, and it would explain why I didn't die in my early twenties like every other poor sap unlucky enough to get called for this job. "He just said something kinda weird." Really, shitbird? Is that the best you can come up with? Worse yet… it was clear from the look on her face that she wasn't gonna let me get away with that one either.

"Mac?"

I felt like my head might explode from the confusion. Here I was, sitting next to this unbelievably beautiful woman that *wants* to know what's in my head and why it's messing with me. All I have to do is tell her and I can't because… shit…

how do you tell someone like her that you're a monster and you didn't even know it? And at the same time, I'm a fuckin idiot. She's a manticore! It's not gonna phase her... hell, she's probably known the whole time.

"Baby?"

"He said I'm not human, Belle." Oh fuck. Those were actual words. I lifted the bottle again and took another drink, but her hand was there, tilting the bottle back down and pulling it gently out of my hand. "I can't be some *mons kochma* after my whole life being..." Being what? I was choking on tears I didn't realize, until that moment, were even trying to fall.

"You don't cause nightmares, Mac." She twisted her fingers through mine and waited until I finally looked over at her. "You banish them."

I shook my head. I'm sure she was trying to make me feel better about it: trying to give me some sort of reason not to let it force me to drink myself into oblivion (not that it would work, mind you - I'd tried on many occasions). "It's not that simple, *nanm mwen*."

"Why not?"

"What?"

"Why *isn't* it that simple, Mac?"

God help me, she was serious.

"*Who* you are isn't defined by the outer shell, love. You, of all people, shouldn't have a problem grasping that."

"I'm not *people*, Belle." My voice was louder. Angry. But I didn't feel angry... just frustrated and confused.

"Am I?"

"What?"

"Am I people, Mac?" She picked up my hand and set it on her chest just below her neck. "Me. Am *I* people?"

"Don't do this, *cheri*."

"Answer me."

She already knew the answer and I knew where she was headed with the whole thing, but that didn't make it any better.

"Yes, Belle. You are people. You have always been people." I pulled my hand away from her chest and used it to bring hers to my lips. "My people."

"If I'm people, Alex, you're people." She smiled a little and stood up, tugging my hand gently. "Now we just have to figure out what type."

$$\sim 13 \sim$$

The next few days were a weird contented sort of blur.

Belle randomly asked questions of me as she worked through the problem of my true nature. I knew it wasn't really random: that she was systematically working through checklist after checklist in her mind trying to narrow down the possibilities based on various traits I'd displayed throughout my life. Personally, I would've been content to sit in the living room, in the dark, and drink myself into a coma but Belle wouldn't allow it. She was driven to provide me with answers she knew I needed even though neither of us knew with any certainty what those answers might look like in the end.

I tried to remain focused and attentive, but Belle was much better at it than I was. She always had been. As soon as I started to spiral, she'd bring me back: she'd take action sometimes before I even realized I needed it. That was nothing new, though. She'd always been my rock. My North star.

I'd just answered some other not-really-random question so I walked up behind her, wrapped my arms around her waist, and buried my face in her hair. "I am so lucky to have you, *nanm mwen.*"

She turned in my arms and leaned her head against my shoulder. "We'll figure this out, Mac. I promise."

"I know, baby."

Do you ever get the feeling that something's too good to be true: that whatever situation you're in is about to blow up in your face?

I got a wave of that just before the pain shot through my head.

Just before the phone rang.

I let my arms fall and took a step back, leaving Belle shaking her head. "Don't answer it."

The thick metallic sludge of blood in my throat made me shake my head. "I can't do that, baby." And the spike in my head made it all the more painful to argue and all the more pressing that I answer that I answer the call.

It seemed like it took forever to find the damned phone but I'm pretty sure that was just because I was in so much pain. I never thought I'd actually like it better when they called in the middle of the night but, apparently, being asleep when it started dulled the effects a bit.

I didn't bother saying hello when I answered. There was no point. The overseers didn't call with information the way normal people call. Come to think of it, there wasn't much about the overseers that was really very normal at all. The phone was just a delivery tool: a mechanism to transfer information from one point to another and it was easier to send that information through direct channels than risk miscommunication due to the use of something so primitive as speech.

I set the phone down and the pain faded to its normal post-notification levels. The situation didn't make any sense but, to be fair, that was usually when they called me.

Belle was pacing the length of the couch when I managed to make my way to the living room. There was one trinket that had a permanent place there: a desktop sized version of Eriksen's *The Little Mermaid* that Nikolai and Coralia had gifted me years ago, infused with spells to help heal minor wounds and ease the pain of the overseers' communication methods. I managed to walk (rather than stumble) to the shelf where the statue sat and set the palm of my hand against the stone base. The relief was never complete, but it was immediate.

"What's the job?"

She was trying to look calm but her eyes betrayed her. I couldn't remember her ever being actually scared by a call coming in before... but kind of a lot had happened since the last time an actual call came in. An honest answer wasn't going to do anything to ease her fear, but what else could I do?

"Pack of hellhounds." I hoped to sound casual and help her relax but somewhere along the line it backfired. Probably something to do with the fact that

"Hellhounds aren't pack animals. Mac!"

"I know, Belle." The pain had subsided to a tolerable level and I pulled my hand away from the statue and walked over to her. "But that's what they sent." I took her hands in mine and squeezed them gently. "I have to go to work, *nanm mwen.*"

"I don't like it, Mac." That much was already clear: she wasn't happy about it at all, but she knew - just like I did - that I didn't have any other options. Not at this point, at least.

"I don't either, baby." I pulled her into my arms. "Quite frankly, it stinks like week-old gas station sushi."

"But you're going, anyway."

I kissed her softly. "You find out a way for me to ignore them without my internal organs melting in reverse-alphabetical order and I will never answer another phone call." And after years of answering impossible calls because they thought I was immortal or something... after years of going after everything they pointed me at because I thought I needed to in order to help someone I'd never even met... I actually meant it.

And she knew it.

I could see it in her eyes: a whole new level of dedication to finding out what I actually was... because that, we both knew, would be the first step in finding out how to finally force them to leave me alone. "I'll help you get ready." Her voice was soft. A little scared.

"I hope so." I kissed her again and the tension in her body melted a tiny bit.

There were a number of reasons I really did want her help, too.

I needed her to feel like she had some control of how I went into this. I needed her expertise. But more than anything... I needed to just be with her as much as I possibly could.

And it didn't take nearly as long as I'd hoped to be armed and ready to go. I asked if she wanted to go with me but she declined: said I could handle a couple troublesome mutts without her help. I wasn't so sure but I didn't argue: I was pretty sure her decision had less to do with her faith in my ability and a whole lot more to do with not wanting to see me get hurt - or worse - again. And while I would have loved to have her with me, both for backup and emotional support, I couldn't even bring myself to ask again once she'd declined... I just couldn't push the issue.

The prep went quick. I didn't want to leave but the sooner I dealt with the hellhounds, the sooner I could come home. We agreed that I had everything I needed so there was no need for a trip to the beach house. Belle kissed me at the garage door.

"Be safe, Mac. Come home to me."

It wasn't far to the last known location of the hounds. If anything, it was too close to home. Less than fifteen miles from the house: a quick run for a hellhound. Luckily, it was a quicker drive for me. There was really no reason to assume they'd target the house, of course... except that there wasn't any reason not to and the way things had been going, I didn't feel much like leaving things to chance.

I parked across the street from the address and surveyed the scene. It was a fairly standard 'creepy old house' but nothing extreme or out of my realm of ordinary… which, I suppose, doesn't say a whole lot about the normalcy of the place. Either way… it didn't look like a doghouse for a bunch of hellhounds.

I got out of the truck, half expecting my nemesis to wave from the house's front door. I wasn't sure that *nemesis* was really the right word for him, but we still didn't know who or what he was… and he had started out with killing me, so that kind of set the tone for our relationship.

But he didn't come through the door. No one came through the door. Nothing from the house at all… not even so much as a light coming on or going out. I walked up the sidewalk about halfway to the corner then turned back and went the same distance from my truck the other way. Still nothing. One more thing (at least) to add to all that just wasn't right with this situation.

"Here, Cujo…"

There had to be *something* here.

There was a cracking sound behind me: the sound of something breaking… somewhere between a branch and a bone. I turned toward the sound with my hand on the hilt of the Ubojica. "I can't believe you answered to Cujo. I mean… seriously, dude?"

The creature cocked its head to one side and regarded me with what I can only describe as disdain. At least I'm pretty sure what the look meant. It was huge, gnarled, and covered in black fur that was slick with… well… something I really didn't even want to guess the origin of. Its blocky head was neatly proportioned to its body, which was roughly the height of a great dane with the build of bull terrier, and its eyes were like a couple hot coals sunk in its head.

"Are we gonna do this or what?"

Two things occurred to me as I taunted the beast. The first was that this thing, according to the report I'd received, wasn't alone. The second thing was that, regardless of how many of them there were, I'd never actually tangled with a hellhound before.

"I am too old for this shit."

The beast lunged toward me and I twisted to the side. It pulled back to regroup: its eyes locked on me while it circled. Locked on my hand. More appropriately, locked on the hilt of the Ubojica. I was wracking my brain trying to remember the nature of the enchantment on the weapon: it had been so long since the source of its power had been an issue that I'd actually forgotten. Was it some angelic infusion rather than regular magic? I just couldn't remember. In my defense, it had been thirty years since I'd had all the details drilled into my head and I'd actively been trying to forget it all for the last twenty.

It lunged again. I dodged again. Maybe it was a dance and I just couldn't hear the music. The gnashing teeth kinda made me think not, but things were just weird enough that I wasn't writing anything off completely.

The hound turned and attacked again. It wasn't getting any faster and it didn't seem to be changing up its tactics but, like everything else, I wasn't taking anything at face value. Belle had reminded me, repeatedly, that hellhounds were extremely intelligent and should never be underestimated. In fact, she'd repeated it: almost like she expected me to take for granted that the hound's clumsy attack was actually indicative of its ability rather than a clever ruse to stroke my ego and set me up to make an idiot mistake.

Because… y'know… why wouldn't I be that idiot?

The hound lunged again, and I dodged again but the beast turned quickly, altering its attack, and snapped at my arm. Its teeth tore through my jacket sleeve but managed to narrowly miss actually tearing flesh. "Son of a…" Nah. Too easy. It drew back and snarled and that's when I knew I'd screwed up.

While this dude had been keeping me busy the rest of its buddies had joined the party and I didn't even see them come in. There was only one direction that wasn't filled with ominous growling: right behind me. There were no hounds between me and my truck. There was, however, far too much ground for me to cover without at least one of them getting to me before I could get to safety.

"Was it the Cujo thing?" I was moving as slowly as I could manage without screwing up my balance and making my situation a million times worse. "Because it seems like it was a bad call on my part." I'd managed a full step back but they'd easily closed the same distance and the last remnants of hope that I'd actually be able to get into the cab of the truck were fading fast. "And I don't even know your mom, so…"

The one that had managed to snag my jacket was inching closer, watching me carefully but behaving a little less aggressively than before. Belle's warning echoed in my mind again: sure, I was playing dumb and the hound seemed to be buying it… but how much of that was just to let me think I had a snowball's chance of getting out of this in one piece? And how much of this second-guessing was just me second-guessing my chances of getting home?

"C'mon, man. Let's talk this out. What's the deal here?"

I wasn't sure if I expected it to answer or not but, when I was surprised to hear a voice in the growling, I figured I hadn't really expected it after all.

"Hungry."

Of course, they were. And their hunger wasn't the kind a bag of Alpo was going to satisfy.

"Why here? Why now?" *Why a pack of you bastards in my territory?*

"Revolution."

"Revolution?" *Why was it that lately, the longer I talked to anything from the other side, the more confused I got?*

"Mmm."

"I'm sorry… but what revolution?" *What the hell are you talking about, Cujo?*

Several of the other hounds growled and the one I was talking to nodded his blocky gnarled head. "Not your concern."

Dude. Don't be difficult. "I gotta disagree with you there… because if you're coming here, as a *pack*, to find a new feeding ground…" I waved around vaguely. "This place? This place *is* my concern."

The hounds growled and snarled amongst themselves: discussing whether I was a legitimate threat or a tasty snack, if I had to guess. The odds really weren't in my favor either way, but that wasn't going to change much of anything. They had to leave, no matter what they decided, and it was up to me to make sure they did. It would be a hell of a lot easier if they were cooperative, though.

"We go."

"Excuse me?" *It couldn't possibly be that easy.*

Cujo nodded slowly. "We honor your… role here." The other hounds began to back away from me. "We go."

I nodded. *What the hell was my* role *that they were honoring?* Again: the longer I spent talking to them, the more confused I got. I was kind of glad they'd just agreed to up and leave. I might be able to retain a shred of sanity after tonight. "Good luck."

I climbed into the cab of the truck as the hounds vanished into the night. I needed to get home: to get all this confusion out of my head and get my body back to something near its normal operating parameters. I locked the doors and closed my eyes: before I could to anything, I had to meditate long enough to be able to drive safely because my brain was running like a dozen methed-up rats in a maze full of dead-ends. My body wasn't much better off, but I could control it enough once I was able to narrow the focus of my brain to the task of getting home.

I managed to drive home, park in the garage, and get the door closed behind me, but that was when my ability to function stopped. Both my mind and body just quit responding: I wasn't dead (again), mind you... just kinda damned-near catatonic. The theory was that it was my body's way of not disintegrating under the physical stress caused by a combination of magic, adrenaline, and the residual effects of being in close proximity to otherworlders: and while it was just a theory, it was the best explanation Nikolai, Coralia, and Belle had come up with over the years.

I forced the last bit of wind out of my lungs, just enough to whisper Belle's name, and then slumped forward on the steering wheel.

I woke in my bed: stripped of my weapons and most of my clothes. My vision was blurred and my body ached down to every last hair follicle. I could smell candles burning, a thick blend of amber and cedar in the air, and - most importantly - the rich cinnamon and vanilla scent that followed Belle everywhere.

"*Bèl larenn mwen an...*"

"You talk too much, Mac." I could hear the fabric of her dress rustling as she walked across the room and felt the bed shift when she sat beside me. "You can't even see, yet, can you?"

"I can see you're worried." She was right, of course: I really couldn't see anything other than dark and light splotches. "And that the hellhounds didn't come here after we were done."

"They're still alive?"

"Yeah." I didn't expect her to sound *that* surprised. "We... um... negotiated?" Even though I still couldn't see her features clearly, I smirked a little knowing Belle was either amused or irritated by my calling any confrontation with *others* a negotiation. "But they said they... um..." If I could remember Cujo's exact words, it might give Belle some insight into what had happened or (maybe more selfishly important) what the hell I was. "They said they honored my role? I think?"

"Your role?" Her tone of voice shifted so drastically I was suddenly far more concerned about it than I'd been to this point. "That's what they said?"

"Yeah." Why did it bother her so much? "I mean... that's what the leader said but it was like they kinda... struggled... coming up with the word. Belle? Baby, what's going on?"

"I don't know yet." I felt her lips on mine and stray wisps of her hair brush my face and neck. "Rest, *cintaku*. Let me worry about this."

I wanted to argue: to help come up with the answers I needed. We needed. But I couldn't find the strength to do it. In fact, now that I'd woken up, all I could really feel was that I felt like I was going to pass out. "You drugged me?"

"I medicated you to ensure you rested properly to heal." She kissed me again.

I wanted to laugh but couldn't quite manage it. "You drugged me."

"I drugged you." I could hear laughter in her voice and the sound washed away everything else. "Get some sleep, Mac."

Apparently, I didn't have a choice.

~14~

I have no idea how long I was out. It only felt like a few minutes but I woke up rested and clear-headed: rather like being in that moment where you turn to the anesthesiologist to tell them you don't think it worked and they tell you the surgery went well. Belle was snuggled in the bed beside me with her arm draped over my stomach and her head laying on my chest. I reached up and let my hand rest on her shoulder, completely content to lay here like this for as long as it took her to wake up.

That quiet moment of bliss, though, ended almost as soon as it began.

Belle stirred when I touched her shoulder and made a sleepy contented sound that made getting *out* of bed pretty much the last thing on my priority list. As my luck would have it, though, I wasn't the one that got to set my priority list.

After that split second of relaxed stillness, Belle pushed herself up on her hands. Her face hung in the air above me, her hair falling around us to create a soft shiny brown barrier between us and the rest of the world.

"Why did you call me your queen earlier?" There was concern in her voice. Fear. Definitely not the sound I expected to be paired with the question.

"I've done that before." Hadn't I?

"No, you haven't." She was anxious. Nervous.

"Well, I should have." Why was she so worried about it?

"Why now, Mac?"

"Belle?" I lifted both my hands to cradle her face. "What is wrong, *cheri*?"

"Tell me exactly what happened with the hounds."

I thought we'd already been through it but there was such concern in her voice, so much fear in her eyes, that I repeated the story. Again. I asked her a few times, as I gave her every detail I could think of from my encounter with the hounds, why she was so concerned with what I'd called her. When she was finally satisfied with the details of the encounter, she took a deep breath and closed her eyes.

"There isn't a species of hound alive that gives a shit about the *role* of any being outside their clan, Mac." I started to repeat the part about how they were in exile because of some revolution but she didn't let me. "And the species you described doesn't even comprehend roles like that. They're blindly and brutally hierarchical. You said it struggled for the word and I think that's because the word it was looking for was sovereignty."

I knew she understood where she thought she was going but trying to describe anything about me with a word like sovereignty was really nothing short of ridiculous. "I don't..."

"When you claimed this place, Mac, they *recognized* that claim. They saw evidence of ascension."

"Fatal flaw in your explanation, Belle..." I shook my head. When powerful beings from the other sides rose, normally through conflict, to rule over their realms it was called ascension. The only problem with her theory was "Humans don't ascend."

"And you're not human." Yeah. I was still having trouble accepting that part. "So put the pieces together, Mac."

"Babe, I..." I was trying to put the pieces together but it felt like I was still missing a few.

"When you went and saved the boy."

"No." I shook my head. "There wasn't even any real confrontation. It was..."

"An abdication."

"Wha..? No..." I started replaying the encounter with my nemesis in my head almost immediately.

"Think about it, Mac." She was certain of her conclusion, that much was obvious from the tone of her voice and the look on her face. "He wanted you out of his way and when you clearly explained why you couldn't go, he tipped his hat and left. He gave you command and somehow, somewhere in your subconscious, you knew it." I was shaking my head. I wanted to tell her that she was grasping at straws and that, if she really thought about it, what she was saying made zero sense... but I couldn't say any of it. "You knew it. And you knew the hounds would back off if you claimed this realm."

I finally managed to force sound from my lips but the words that came out weren't the argument I'd been trying for. "And because I'm the sovereign now, that makes you my queen and as I was passing out I had to make sure you knew it, too." As soon as the words started, I wanted to clamp my teeth shut but this was, apparently, one of those times when I was actually physically incapable of shutting up.

"You understand."

"No! No, Belle, I don't understand!" It had been almost ten years since I'd had an anxiety attack but the symptoms were unmistakable. I squeezed my eyes shut, took a few deep breaths and started pushing through the mental exercises that were supposed to help me regain control of the emotional rollercoaster. "I don't understand."

She laid down on top of me with her head on my shoulder: adding the weight of her body to the various methods I was using to keep from spiraling down a very bad path. Cinnamon and vanilla overpowered all the other scents in the room.

"Think about it, Mac." Her voice was soothing and managed to break through the roar of my blood rushing through my veins. "This could be what you've been waiting for."

"What are you talking about?"

"If you're the sovereign, all the players in this realm have to submit to your will, right?"

"I... I guess so, yeah." I still had no clue what she was getting at, but her voice was so calm and relaxed that I knew she thought she had the ultimate answer to something. And I certainly didn't mind listening to her.

Her body shifted. Her lips brushed mine. "That means the overseers have to submit, too."

All the implications of her simple statement took a lot more processing time than they should have but when it finally started to come together, I wrapped my arms around her. "Can it really be that easy?"

"I doubt it will be easy, Mac." She kissed me again. "But it will be worth it."

~15~

Now that Belle had decided she had all the answers, it was time to start poking holes in her theories. Not that I wanted to, mind you: the thought of being able to finally tell the overseers to fuck off and having them be forced to listen was pretty damned attractive, after all. But in order for it to work, we still needed to know what I was and how I'd somehow ended up in the line of succession. Neither of which was going to be as simple as it sounded.

Especially considering we didn't really have anywhere to start.

"That's not entirely true, Mac."

"Really?" Belle had told me, many times, that I didn't even need my voice to communicate: that my facial expressions were enough to convey whatever thoughts might be going through my mind. I didn't always believe her, but this time I did. Of course, her reaction to my expression still didn't shut me up. "What do we have, Belle?" I was doing it again. I took a deep breath and tried to soften my tone. "The word of the thing that killed me and the fact that a bunch of hellhounds tucked tail and took off when I told them to?"

"And how the hell is that second one *not* enough for you to take this seriously?"

"Serious isn't the problem, Belle. God! The one thing I've been after from the overseers for years is finally *maybe* within reach! Serious is definitely not the problem."

"Then what is?" She was getting tired of trying to keep me going. I could tell. She'd never complain about it, of course, but I certainly couldn't hold her fatigue against her. Hell, on my good days I was a pain in the ass… and the last couple days definitely hadn't been good ones.

"Damn it, Belle, it just doesn't make any fuckin sense!"

She laughed. Not a chuckle. Not a giggle. The same deep paralyzing sort of laughter I'd suffered when my nemesis said he wanted me to retire. It took her a moment to recover but when she did, she took a deep breath and shook her head.

"Alex Vantanpèt McLaren, what part of your life has *ever* made sense?"

I don't think anyone had said my middle name out loud since mine and Stefanie's wedding. It was disturbing and exhilarating at the same time, but also a little sobering. It was almost that feeling of knowing you're in trouble when you get called your full name… but not quite. There was something different about it. I reached across the table and took her hands. "Belle, *Rèn mwen*, the only part of my life that makes any sort of sense at all is knowing that I don't deserve either of the women who've loved me."

She smiled and laughed. "That wasn't exactly what I was asking, Mac."

"*Okontrè, cheri*, that is *exactly* what you asked." I knew she wasn't going to let me off the hook, but I could at least take the opportunity to remind her of how completely amazing she was… if only for the fleeting moment before she went all-business again.

"Will you *please* be serious?" She held a finger up to silence me before I could argue that I was being completely serious. "This is your chance to be free of them, Mac. We just have to figure out the details."

I pulled her hands close to me and set my forehead down on them. I never was one for figuring out details: I'm the one you point at a problem when you want it to go away, not when you want to make sense of it. "Belle, I just don't know what I'm after… I don't know what to look for or where to look for it… it's just…"

"Don't spiral, love." Her voice was calm. Soothing. Grounding.

"How the hell do you do that?"

She just laughed again. I felt her kiss the back of my head. I lifted my head up slowly: nothing like breaking her nose to completely ruin the mood, after all. She had leaned back, though, so everyone returned to sitting upright unharmed.

"I've asked someone for help."

It was a simple statement. One that made sense, even. So why did it immediately put me on edge?

"Who?"

She looked nervous. The only times I'd seen her look nervous were when she was worried about me. "Can we agree that desperate times call for desperate measures?"

The more she danced around the question, the more concerned I was about the answer.

"WHO?" I roared. I didn't raise my voice. I didn't scream. I roared. Like the fucking beast I apparently am. She flinched and, while part of me felt horrible about it, the part that roared didn't even seem to notice. I managed to lower my volume but I apparently couldn't do anything about my tone. "Who the fuck did you call, Belle?"

"Šapat." She was shrinking away from me. Talking fast. She was afraid of me. "I called Šapat."

I hated myself more in that moment than I ever thought possible… and considering how much I hated myself when Stefanie was dying in my arms, that was saying something. I stood up slowly, struggling to keep from letting the rage that was consuming me take control of my body.

"Mac?"

I turned. Too fast. She flinched again. I wanted to claw my eyes out just so I couldn't see how I was scaring her.

"I'm just going downstairs, Belle." My teeth were clenched. I was growling. There were tears in her eyes and I just couldn't fucking stop. "Please don't try to stop me."

She whimpered and nodded and took a step back.

I slammed open the door that led to the basement and slammed it closed behind me. The stairs were narrow and dark and had been in need of repair for some time but right now I didn't care about any of that. If I fell down the stairs and broke my neck on the cement floor, it wouldn't be a loss to anyone. Not right now, anyway. The loss of this bastard rage-beast would only make the world a better place. The stairs held, though, and I didn't tumble to my death this time. Too bad.

I yanked the pull-cord on the overhead light and the thin beaded chain came off in my hand. I snarled and threw the cord across the basement then moved toward the weights. Part of my brain was still working on the problem of what I was: noting with an almost clinical detachment that, if I were human, my eyes wouldn't have adjusted so quickly to the underground darkness. I wouldn't have been stacking every weight I could find on the bars, either: if I were human. I only had a little over six hundred in plates that would fit the bar so I laid down on the bench and lifted the bar. If I were human, I wouldn't have had a chance to lift it at all. Not with my build. Another point in the monster's favor, I guess. After that, my plan was simple: I would lift until I burned through the rage and was able to control myself again or I was going to keep going until my arms turned to jelly and I dropped the damned bar on my face or throat. Either way, the beast wasn't going back up those stairs.

Once my head started to clear I was able to concede that asking Šapat for assistance made sense.

She'd been one of the overseers when I was first called and had disconnected herself from the collective the first time they called me back. She had been extremely vocal in her opposition to their not allowing me to live the peaceful life I'd fought so hard for: she'd been my only champion on that council. But the fact that she had been part of that council at all was what had made the rage explode: the fact that hers had been one of the voices that set me on this path.

I could feel myself starting to sweat. That was good. That meant I was actually burning through... well... something. Right?

I could hear sounds upstairs. Voices. Belle and Šapat. I wondered if I could hear them if I tried: if whatever had allowed my eyes to adjust to the darkness of the basement had enhanced my hearing as well. Maybe that was why the sound of my blood rushing through my veins was so damned loud. I decided I probably could hear them if I tried but, in the end, it seemed better not to try. If the thought of having someone else involved in finding the answer to what I was had made me as crazy as I had been when I came down here, eavesdropping on the discussion wasn't likely to help matters.

Besides: if I wasn't trying to listen to them, I could let my mind work on the problem, too. Not that I really expected to come up with anything... hell, there were days lately I felt like I wouldn't know my own name if Belle didn't say it.

I pushed harder with the weights when I thought about Belle: about the way she flinched when I roared and backed away when I stood up... she probably flinched when I slammed the door open and shut, too. I'd watched my mother flinch like that and, even as a kid, I swore I'd never be responsible for making anyone feel that way. I'd even prided myself in the fact that even though I was a drunk (and I knew it), the only things I'd ever abused were alcohol and my truck. My stepfather's voice - a sound I'd worked long and hard to burn out of my brain over the years - laughed as it reminded me *it's not abuse unless you use your fist.* I roared again (which didn't help my state of mind any) and dropped the bar on the metal stand over my head. The stand squeaked a little under the sudden weight but didn't collapse. I stood up, not sure if the fact that the bar *hadn't* fallen was good or not, and walked across the room to the punching bag. I missed the bag on my first swing and my hand smashed into the unfinished concrete wall.

The wall, thankfully, didn't crack or crumble but I wasn't so sure about my knuckles. Dealing with physical pain was something I'd always been able to do even before I was called so the fact that I was still on my feet wasn't too surprising. What was surprising, though, was that I was actually smart enough not to hit the wall again. Remember when I said you point me at problems you want to go away? Yeah… that's how I'm wired. I don't stop until I'm done and, in this moment, I was nowhere near done hating myself up for becoming the abusive asshole I swore I'd never become… but I stopped hitting the wall. I stopped hitting anything. I didn't even want to hit anything.

Maybe that meant the rage was subsiding.

I shook my head and turned toward the stairs. I would decide before I got to the door if I could trust myself to walk through it or not. I was only really certain of one thing: I wasn't leaving the basement unless I knew, without a doubt, that I would give Belle no reason to flinch or be afraid of me again.

I paused at the door: hesitated and second-guessed my ability to behave a couple times before reaching for the doorknob with my uninjured hand. I opened the door slowly. I tried to tell myself it was because I had no idea where the women on the other side of the door were at the moment but I knew the truth: my actions had to prove I could be trusted. A simple verbal confirmation that I'd calmed down wasn't going to cut it.

Nor should it.

See… not only had I seen my mother flinch like that… seen that same fear in my mother's eyes… but I'd seen the aftermath. I knew all the tearful excuses, seen the caked-on make-up, heard the hushed pleas not to make him angry…

It was all playing back in my mind except, this time, I was the monster in the story.

Not being human was no excuse.

I had to prove it.

To both of us.

The women were sitting at the table drinking coffee. Whatever conversation they were having when the door opened stopped suddenly and I didn't blame them. They had no idea what was going to come up from the basement, after all, and I had no idea how much Belle had been able or willing to share with Šapat about what had happened just before her arrival.

I bowed to Šapat as I approached. "Welcome, *visoka.*[8]"

You have to understand, I'm pretty sure this woman was young when Martin Luther was hanging his list of the church's offenses on its door. She was

---

[8] Exalted lady

old, deeply benevolent, incredibly wise, immeasurably powerful… basically like a supernatural RBG… and she was sitting at my kitchen table drinking coffee with my girlfriend.

When Šapat nodded her acknowledgement of my greeting I turned away from her almost immediately. I really wasn't trying to offend her and, in the back of my mind, I hoped that seeing *why* I turned so suddenly would grant me some tiny measure of forgiveness for my rudeness.

I fell on my knees at Belle's chair and dropped my head. "*Trezò mwen,* I have no right to ask forgiveness for my behavior. And I know you have no reason to trust my words *nanm mwen,* but I swear to you it will never happen again."

"I forgive you, *cintaku.*" Belle's voice was soft but, thankfully, strong and unwavering. She lifted my face gently and I kissed her hand. "And I do believe y… oh my God, Mac! Your hand!"

I had been so focused on my apology that I had actually forgotten the fact that I was holding my injured hand against my chest but, when Belle reached down and lifted my face, she caught sight of the mangled sack of skin and splintered bone. I wanted to make some sort of joke just to give her back that moment of peace but I couldn't manage it. In fact, now that it was in the front of my mind, even my normal abnormally high pain tolerance wasn't helping much. "It looks worse in the light." The joke didn't do much for any of us. I don't know if it actually felt worse suddenly or if it was the ability to see, in detail, the splintered bits of bone poking through the skin in places where I should have knuckles but I was suddenly nauseous and dizzy.

It was all kind of a blur for a minute. I don't know when she moved but suddenly Belle was beside me, easing my body to the floor and resting my head in her lap. She wiped sweat from my forehead with her sleeve and I thought, at first, she was singing but then my brain processed the sounds: a healing chant. Either I passed out momentarily or Šapat teleported to our side (I wouldn't put money either way), but she was there almost immediately; her ancient crone fingertips tracing healing runes along the length of my forearm.

While they had both worked healing magic on me before, this experience was like none other before. It was potent. Raw. Almost feral. I don't think either of them did anything different than they had before, either. It worked, though: better than I ever would have expected. While it wasn't really doing anything for the pain, the damage was being mended as I watched: bones moving back into place, skin knitting, proper color returning.

"The pain will subside, *ratnik*.[9]"

I wasn't sure if the pain was actually subsiding or if I'd just adjusted to the new level but, either way, I nodded. "I am in your debt, Šapat." I looked up at Belle's face and forced a smile. "And you, *mwen chè*. You, I owe everything."

Šapat rose to her feet with the ease and grace of a dancer, her long skirt billowing like the fluttering edges of jellyfish lazily whooshing their way through the aquarium display I'd seen years ago. Lifetimes ago, it felt like.

"Often have I heard that promise made to me." Šapat laughed as she sat back down at the kitchen table. "Never from the *kraljevski*.[10]"

"Not you, too."

The old woman laughed again and patted the tabletop. "Come off from the floor, children. Sit with me and, together, we will find the truth of it all."

I sat up too fast and sent my head spinning. Belle was right there: her hands on my shoulders, steadying me. "Easy, Mac." She guided me to one of the chairs. "You need water."

I needed whiskey but I wasn't going to argue with her right now.

"*Belle* tells me you died." Šapat wasn't one to beat around the bush. And of course, she didn't say Belle: she used her actual name. "And that after you recovered, you faced again the *svrgnut* and became *uznesen*."

I nodded as Belle set a glass in front of me and sat in the chair beside me. "That's pretty much how *Belle* thinks it all happened."

I'd kind of expected some clapback from Belle about how she couldn't understand that I still didn't buy into it all but it didn't come. Šapat was sitting there smiling and nodding and Belle was staring at me like she had no idea who I even was. Then it occurred to me. I didn't say 'Belle,' either.

"This much answers the question of your heritage, eh *kraljevski?* At least in so much as that you are not fully human."

I was nodding but my head was sinking down into my hands. Up until that moment, I'd been able to convince myself that the nonhuman part of the equation was an error: something that would have an explanation once we found some other pieces and put them in place. Considering a human being is physically incapable of pronouncing half the sounds in the manticore language though, the fact that I'd not only said her name but said it perfectly was a little too much to ignore.

---

[9] Warrior

[10] Royalty

Belle's hand settled lightly on my arm and I looked up. The fear and confusion that had filled her face were gone: only a glimmer of uncertainty left in the deepest places in her eyes.

"*Nanm mwen,* I don't... I can't..."

"Mac." Her voice was soft. Comforting. "Don't."

"Now, Alex McLaren, we find out who you really are."

Until she spoke, I'd almost forgotten Šapat was even sitting there. The whole day was turning into some fucked up dream that didn't make any sense at all: so much so that I was half expecting the table to join the conversation.

"Forgive me, *visoka,* but I don't think it's going to be that easy."

"Everything is that easy, *kraljevski.* If you know what you are doing."

I chuckled and nodded. There were times I really missed that old woman's outlook on life. "And you know what you're doing."

Šapat laughed. "I already know *what* you are, McLaren. The question is, are you ready to learn?"

I didn't feel like I had much of a choice but I wasn't going to say that out loud so I nodded instead.

Šapat turned to Belle and she nodded slightly. "And you? Because you know this can change things."

Change things?! How the hell could this change anything? I wanted to say as much but I couldn't get the words from my brain to my mouth. I watched, feeling helpless, as Belle nodded reverently.

Šapat closed her eyes and nodded.

More than anything, in that moment, I wanted a reset on the last minute or so... just long enough for me to tell the old woman I wasn't ready to hear it: to stop the mad downhill the whole thing seemed to have decided to jump on.

"You, McLaren. You have certain affinity for lion, yes?"

I shrugged. "I'm a Leo."

Šapat scoffed and shook her head. "You are barong ket, McLaren."

"What?!" No. That couldn't be right. It couldn't be right on way too many levels. "I... no..." Belle's hand left my arm and my eyes snapped to her. I was panicked. She was sitting in the chair with her hands in her lap and her eyes on the floor. "No!"

Šapat rose slowly. "Forgive me, *kraljevski.* I will leave you two to discover what this revelation means... for you." And she was gone. Disappeared into thin air.

"Belle?" She didn't move. I wanted to scream but, if it came out a roar, it would only make things worse. "*Belle?*" I wasn't terribly sure saying her name would be much better, but it almost definitely wouldn't be worse.

She nodded but didn't look up, her voice barely louder than a whisper. "*Ya, tuanku?*"

"No." So, I was wrong. It was worse. At least for me. "No, no." I was on my knees in front of her again, my hands wrapping around hers. "*Nanm mwen*, no."

"You are barong ket." She still wasn't looking at me: still barely speaking. "I am not allo…"

"I'm me, Belle." I interrupted her and she didn't scowl. This was insane. I lifted her head and turned mine so that her still-lowered eyes *had* to see my face. "And you, *bèl larenn mwen… nanm presye mwen*, will never be below me." And considering I didn't go for the very obvious innuendo, you know how serious things really were. "*Rèn mwen*, I am yours more than you are mine."

Belle gave a tiny laugh and the corners of her lips rose in the beginning of a smile. "Oh, Mac, I…"

"I know, Belle." I kissed her hands softly then laid my head in her lap. She brushed her fingers through my hair and, for a moment, everything was okay.

See… here's the part you probably don't get about all the craziness that just happened.

The barong ket were the rulers of a huge portion of the otherworld creatures and they ruled for a long time. The problem, of course, is that they were raging assholes.

Family trait, I guess.

There was a rebellion: an uprising against the mistreatment at the hands of the barong ket.

Wanna guess who started it?

Yeah, I didn't think you'd need more than one.

The rebellion was squashed, viciously, and the manticore were thrust into slavery: kept as pets if they were lucky and used as a hell of a lot worse if they weren't.

Belle had every reason to be scared of me after the way I'd behaved and now, we had this wrinkle to iron out. But to her, it all made sense now and all she had to do - in her own mind, at least - was not piss me off. The problem, of course, was that the fact that she even felt like she had to feel that way pissed me off.

Then there was the additional mystery of how she'd actually ended up in my closet all those years ago. If I was barong ket, was she enslaved by my family? Is that why she reacted the way she did? I couldn't ask her... I could barely get her to look at me.

Right now, more than anything, I needed things to be normal with us.

As normal as they got, anyway.

I needed her to be okay with what I was and we needed to figure out what that meant for us. So many things I'd have to control and she'd have to unlearn just to remain ourselves rather than conforming to the expectations of our natures.

We had one thing in our favor, though...

I've never really conformed to anything in my life.

There was at least one unexpected benefit of the super-stressful dynamic that had been layered on top of our relationship: Belle knew damned near everything there was to know about the barong ket. Including a ton of shit the overseers didn't bother to download into my brain.

I spent the day at Belle's side, terrified that I'd lose what little ground I seemed to gain here and there on the road back to where we'd been before the world went to shit this morning.

Because we'd spent nearly my entire life together Belle knew what I did about the barong ket but, more important, she knew what I didn't know.

While we continued through our wild, crazy, unexplainable, wacked-out, shit day, she filled in the blanks on a bunch of things that didn't quite add up.

For starters, barong ket are extremely rare and have been for centuries. Even before the uprising their numbers were extraordinarily low, especially for a race that ruled over so many. Part of the reason was that the otherworld entity didn't mature or actually gain any power until its human host died. In battle. I guess if that's the only way, being a race of raging assholes makes a little more sense. There were rumors of families that escaped the uprising and hid among the humans, avoiding conflict and keeping away from any real dangers in order to maintain their line. Belle thought, perhaps, this might be the case with me... and that, as a side note, for all the dad of the year awards my stepfather never won, he was probably a step-up for my mother if the theory that I was one of these hidden barong ket was true.

And since the barong ket, historically, were royalty (and yes, we did go off on a tangent about Richard the Lionheart and the jury's still out since it was the infection that killed him not the battle), it made sense that my nemesis had abdicated to me rather than some other being in this realm, even if I was a half-breed.

Which still didn't answer the question of why he decided to abdicate to begin with but I had a feeling the only way we'd get an answer to that one was if he dropped in for coffee one day.

And, as Belle found it necessary to remind me, the whole thing about my being a half-breed wasn't necessarily true either. Just because we didn't know if my mother was barong ket didn't mean anything: drinking yourself to death didn't count as a battle, either. Regardless of why you drank.

In the end though, the only thing we'd really established was that I was genetically predisposed to be an asshole. So much for the nurture versus nature question. Belle was basically back to normal, though, in spite of everything. Whatever else this shit had in store for us, at least we got that win.

~16~

I still wasn't sure I bought the whole barong ket thing, in spite of the ridiculous amount of (what I kept trying to write off as circumstantial) evidence in support of it. I really wanted to ask Nikolai about it but I kept coming up with excuses not to go to the beach house. Honestly, I was afraid of what he and Coralia would tell me and ultimately, I wanted reasons not to believe it, not confirmation.

"Do you think they'll call me again? Now that this change is on their radar?"

Belle looked up from the book in her lap. It didn't seem like that strange a question to me, but I was the one that asked it so there's that. The look on her face though… I couldn't quite figure out what she was thinking, but it didn't seem like I was going to like it. Or that she thought I wasn't going to like it, at any rate.

"If they call, tell them no."

"Belle." I shook my head. "You know I can't do that."

"No." Well, that was blunt. "I know the human you couldn't do that."

"But when they called about the hounds…"

"You went."

Yeah, apparently I scowl when I'm interrupted too. Sue me. "Because I had to."

"Did you tell them no?"

She couldn't be serious. They were not gonna let go that easy.

"Did you?"

"No. But…"

"So, try, Mac." She pulled the ribbon down between the pages and set the book aside then walked across the room and sat on my knee. "We didn't know, then, what we do now. You believed they still had control, so they did."

I put my arms around her waist and she leaned against my chest with her head on my shoulder. "You really think they're gonna let me go that easy, *nanm mwen*?"

"I don't know." She sounded like she did know, though, and that knowledge agreed with my outlook. Still, she had decided to cling to hope and who was I to argue? God knew one of us had to be optimistic sometimes. "But neither will you unless you try."

I know I started the conversation but now I really wanted to get away from it. What started as a random thought was turning into one of those make-your-choice-but-choose-wisely type of deals and I was still a little too brain-fried for that.

"You look like you could use a drink."

I chuckled and kissed her softly. "I wouldn't turn one down."

She stood up and smirked at me over her shoulder. "Do you ever?"

"Ouch." She wasn't wrong, but still...

She came back with a bottle of Jack Daniels and a glass. I held the glass while she poured a fairly significant amount. It wouldn't be the first time she'd tried to control my drinking and, with the way things were going, I couldn't blame her for it. But she took the glass and handed me the bottle then sat back down on my knee.

"You okay, Belle?"

She sipped at her glass and nodded.

I took a drink and leaned back in the chair so she could lay against me. I kept waiting for the other shoe to drop: that she found something terrible in her research or that she had sensed something coming that was bound to be trouble or that one of the seers had contacted her about some dire vision of the future. She pulled her feet up and curled up against me. I put my arm around her and kissed the top of her hair. "You sure you're okay?"

"Why wouldn't I be?"

I laughed and kissed her again. "Like there's not a hundred reasons for you not to be okay, right now?"

"Name one."

I was going to start with the whole barong ket thing but just as I started to say it, it occurred to me what she was doing. Clever girl. If she could get me to say all the things I was still trying to deny about myself, then she'd be able to use that as ammunition against my denials later. So, instead, I said "you're in love with an asshole."

She laughed softly and nodded. "Well, that's definitely true."

Damn. I deserved that. Every bit of it, really. But it still stung a little to hear her confirm it.

We sat there in silence for a little while. Even with the little jabs she'd been taking, it was nice to just sit there. It seemed like she was picking at me more than usual: jabbing a little harder than she normally did… but maybe not. Maybe I was just so hyper-sensitive about how I was behaving that I was picking up more of it from her than I normally did. Or maybe, the possibility that I was *barong ket* had triggered some of the centuries-old malice between the two races. Or maybe, I just needed to quit trying to figure out what had caused a change I wasn't even completely sure had occurred.

Peace and quiet never really hung around too long, though.

Honestly, I don't know how much time actually passed. I'd finished about half of what had been in the bottle of Jack when the phone started ringing though.

Belle jumped a little at the sound but I just shook my head. There was no warning: no pain or weakness or puking up blood to herald the call. It was just a phone call. Belle looked at me expectantly and I nodded. I don't think she was asking permission to answer it… not really… just looking for confirmation that she should. At least, that was what I was going to keep telling myself. She unwrapped herself from my arms and walked across the floor to the hook where my still-mangled jacket hung. She fished the phone out of the jacket pocket and scowled at the display before swiping across the screen.

"Hello?" She smiled. "No, they're not available." She held the phone a little away from her ear and smirked. "I'm sorry. I'll let them know you called." Then she swiped the screen again and put the phone back in my jacket pocket, then turned back toward me and grinned.

"Belle?"

She sauntered back across the room and picked up her glass, raising it in a toast. "It seems you're free of their physical chains, at least, *cintaku*."

I should have been happy. Hell, I should have been overjoyed.

"What did they say, Belle?"

"They demanded to speak with you." She shrugged. "I told them you weren't available. They demanded again. I said sorry and hung up." She took a sip of her whiskey and smiled.

"That's it?"

She set her glass down and crawled back into my lap. "That's it."

I set the bottle down on the floor beside the chair and wrapped my arms around her. I wanted her to be right but they'd fucked me over too many times for me to trust that one phone call was going to make them leave me alone. Still, none of the physical signs had preceded the call: that had to mean something.

<h1 style="text-align:center">~17~</h1>

I spent the next week or so feeling like every breath I took was setting me up for the other shoe to drop. I'd been particularly careful to keep the barong ket's rage chained in the deepest parts of my soul: keeping it in reserve for the battles that might call for it rather than letting it be the devil on my shoulder, growling in my ear to just start breaking shit.

Belle had noticed and mentioned it in passing but didn't make as big a deal out of it as I knew she felt it was. She'd been continuing her research on the barong ket, filling in as many blanks as possible for both of us (even though I was still trying to remain in denial), and coming up with dozens of theories as to which family I was descended from and how much of my blood was full-on imperial blue. She was determined, for whatever reason, to prove that I was of *the* imperial barong ket clan.

Personally, I wasn't that interested. I had spent so much of my life just trying to be me in the world, that I really didn't give a damn about anything that came before me. Belle had been with me through it all: my father's disappearance, my struggles trying to live as assigned, my step-father's abuse, my mother's death... all of it was behind me and the last thing I wanted to do was to go even further back and have to stumble through any of that shit again.

Thankfully, because Belle had been with me at least as long as I could remember, she wasn't asking me for a bunch of details and forcing me to revisit shit I had no desire to deal with on any level. She would just casually mention, now and then, that she found some bit of evidence that seemed to confirm her suspicions.

We were sitting in the kitchen, eating lunch, when there was a knock at the front door. This was uncommon for a number of reasons: for one thing, we almost never have visitors. The only people that show up at the house without notice are Sammy and, on very rare occasions, Nikolai. After Stefanie died, I had earned the *mean drunk widow* reputation with the neighbors: not underserved by any stretch of the imagination but it kept the random visitors to basically zero. Even the door-to-door salvation peddlers had quit knocking: apparently offering to help speed things along so they can find out first-hand if they're right about God puts you on a no-knock list. Who knew? Anyway… the point is… people don't randomly knock on my door in the middle of the day.

Belle was already on her feet and heading toward the door when my brain finally processed the bigger picture. I reached out and grabbed her arm as she started to walk past me: too fast and too tightly, I realized too late. She flinched and I wanted to sink through the floor.

"Let me."

She nodded and tried her best to swallow the fear on her face and make it seem like everything was okay. It wasn't and I knew it, but I had to deal with whoever was at the door before I could do anything else. Why was it so damned hard to keep the beast caged?

I walked to the front of the house, trying to maintain enough control so that I didn't actually hurt whoever it was that hadn't got the memo about not coming to my door. I pulled open the door and glared at the kid on the porch: looked to be male, about sixteen, dressed like he wanted to play the hip-hop card but his mom wouldn't let him out of the house dressed like that so he had to improvise. There was something else, though: something no one that didn't know what they were looking for would have noticed.

"Wrong house, *chasè*."

The kid shook his head and took a step forward. "I don't think so."

The overseers' other shoe had dropped. They'd activated their next hunter and sent him after me. If I wasn't being forced to fight a kid who was being puppet mastered to kill me or die trying, I might have laughed at the situation. The one asset they'd never been able to quit falling back on was now a target… how cliche could a committee of dubious origin and questionable morality get?

I had to talk this kid down and I needed to do it *before* I lost control of the beast.

"Look, kid. You don't wanna do this."

The kid reached behind his back - going for a blade, I knew - and shook his head. "Doesn't really matter what I want, does it?" His blade was brand new: clean and shiny. None of the visible wear that made the Ubojica such an intimidating piece of weaponry. "Can't have monsters like you running around."

I laughed. I couldn't help it. "You ain't seen monster yet, son." I took a step back and rolled my shoulders. "And trust me, you don't want to."

The kid wasn't quite as keen on actually coming through the door which was actually what I'd been hoping for. If I could keep enough distance between us that he couldn't get a meaningful attack in, I could probably keep the beast in check… and if I couldn't, I might be able to get far enough inside for Belle to save the kid before the beast did something that would end up killing me later.

"Why you runnin, monster?"

"To save your ass, kid."

He took a step forward. God damn it, kid, don't do it.

"I'm not afraid of you."

"You should be." I took another step back. Gotta keep some distance between us. "Hell, I am."

"Afraid of me?"

I laughed again. Louder. It sounded monstrous even to my ears. "No, kid." Please, hear this Belle. Please come save this kid. "I'm afraid of me."

"They said a beast like you can't be left alive."

The kid was wavering a little bit: trying to reconcile the download with what was actually happening. I wondered how many times I'd been sent out, particularly in those first few years, with faulty information. How many so-called beasts I'd killed on their say-so. And why didn't I question it? This kid, at least, was hesitating.

"Did they tell you why?" My voice didn't even sound like my voice. Part of me kinda wished there was a mirror in the hall just to see how much of the barong ket (if that's what I was) was actually showing but, considering I was probably too old at this point to look like Lion-o, I settled for the fact that I could remain in denial if I couldn't actually see the beast. "Or did they just tell you… fuck, what's the line… a threat to the safety of innocents? Inherently evil?"

I could see it in his face: that's exactly what they told him. The standard excuse. The one that didn't need explanation or evidence.

"That's it, isn't it?" God, I wanted this to end. I couldn't stand the sound of my voice and it felt like every inch of my skin was on fire. "They didn't tell you I used to be you, did they?"

There it was. The kid stopped moving forward, lowered the blade slightly. "What?"

"That's right." Belle. She was walking in from the living room: putting herself between me and the kid. "Go back and ask them about Alex McLaren."

The kid looked at Belle but never quite took his eyes off me. I had to give him credit: he was being at least half smart about it. "Are you alright, miss?"

Belle smiled and nodded. She was trying to look calm and relaxed but she was scared and it showed, at least to me. If the kid and I had anything in common, he was going to see it too and reach a completely different conclusion and the whole thing could turn real bad, real quick.

The kid looked a little more closely at Belle. Okay, a *lot* more closely. I watched him examine her expression. Her stance. And I saw it the same time he did: discolored skin peeking out from under the edge of her sleeve. I'd bruised her arm when I reached out to stop her from answering the door. Fuck.

"Are you sure?"

It wasn't going to help the case the kid was building against me in his head but I took a step back anyway. I really didn't want to get into it with the kid: not ever, really, but especially not while I was trying to figure out how to keep the rage-beast under control. The last thing I wanted to do was kill some kid who'd been sucked in and twisted the same way I had.

"Everything's fine."

Damn it, Belle, that's not what he asked. She was nervous. Of course she was nervous. But the kid was going to come to the same conclusion I would have in his shoes: the monster he'd been sent to kill had been holding and torturing this woman.

I took another slow step back. If I could get a door between me and the kid, I could figure out a way to get out of the house. Then I could try to make sense of the rest of it. But I had to not kill the kid first. I managed another couple steps while the kid tried to figure out just how much trouble Belle was in and if it was more important to kill me or get her out. I was really hoping this was where the kid and me differed and that he'd grab her and run, then come back to kill me when she was safe. I was never that compassionate: kinda makes me wonder how many of the people I saved over the years are still in therapy.

The kid was quick: I had to give him that. He put himself between Belle and I and glared at me. He was set in a good stance: light on his feet with his weapon ready. I wanted to tell him to take her and go: to let him think he'd won this round and rescued the damsel in distress. If he was busy rescuing Belle, he didn't have time for me to kill him. It was all a great theory except for one problem.

What came out of my mouth was a snarling, roaring, "HOW DARE YOU?!"

Yeah. This definitely wasn't going to go the way I wanted it to.

The kid backed up, basically herding Belle toward the door. This could still work.

"I'll be back for you, monster."

The kid ushered Belle out the front door and then they were gone.

I managed to fight off the urge to follow them but just barely. I needed to get myself under control before I did anything else. But how the hell was I supposed to do that? The only way I'd successfully calmed myself down in more than twenty years was by drinking myself into a coma and I didn't know how this thing I had become would react to that: if I lost control completely instead of cooling off, what would happen? Belle could tell me: but she wasn't here. The kid had rescued her.

Oh God.

Belle wasn't here.

The kid had rescued her.

What if she didn't come back?

Oh shit.

What was I going to do if she didn't come back?!

I couldn't remember a time when she wasn't there: first to keep me company, then to help guide me, and now... what if she didn't come back?! What if, when the kid took her out of here, she actually chose to take the opportunity to get away from the monster I'd become?

Don't do this. Don't spiral like this. My voice wasn't cutting it and I couldn't imagine hers. Seriously not helping. I stumbled to the entrance to the living room and caught my reflection in the mirror over the fireplace. Definitely some kind of lionesque monster. Definitely *not* Lion-o. At this point, though, it didn't matter. I bee-lined for the liquor cabinet and grabbed the bottle closest to my hand.

I didn't bother looking at the label and didn't really taste it as I poured it straight down my throat.

The same with the next bottle.

And the next.

By the fourth bottle I slowed down enough to, at least, look at what was in my hand before I started chugging it. It was one of the many imported vodkas Nik had gifted me with over the years: apparently pretty good stuff if you like the taste of vodka, if I recalled correctly. It worked for me, though. Somewhere about the half-way point, I blacked out.

~18~

The voice I heard when I started to come to wasn't the voice I wanted to
hear but, all things considered, it was probably the one I really *needed* to hear.
My eyes weren't even open yet but my mind could already see him fussing over
some concoction while he muttered.

"Alex, you fool. What have you done, huh? You trying to kill yourself?"

"The thought has crossed my mind once or twice."

I managed to force my eyes open about the time Nikolai turned around.

"You live through this one, huh? What is it, now? Five alcohol poisonings?" I
didn't realize anyone was counting. "You're not Rasputin, are you?"

He was chuckling. Not for long.

"I dunno. Was he barong ket, too?"

"No, he was... what?" I knew that would make him stop laughing. He
scowled a little as he walked toward me. "What gave you that idea?"

"Šapat, actually." I thought I was going to sit up but my body decided
otherwise. As soon as I started to move, my head started pounding and the
room started to spin. At least I hadn't had to have my stomach pumped this
time. I leaned back and set my head back down on the floor.

"You called Šapat?"

"Belle called Šapat." It all rushed back: how I'd over-reacted, lost control of
the beast... lost everything. I didn't know if I should thank the stress or the
booze for the wave of nausea that threatened to make a rancid mess of my living
room carpet. I was shaking: struggling to breathe. Anxiety. Again. Jesus Christ,
was this really necessary?

"Alex?" Nikolai knelt beside me. "Stay with me."

I closed my eyes. I couldn't see worth a damn with the room spinning
anyway: I might as well try to fight the tears. "She's gone, Nik." I felt his hand on
my shoulder. He was in the house: he knew she was gone. What the hell was my
problem? "I turned into a fuckin monster and she's gone. I lost her." I was

choking on the tears I was trying to fight and figured it would probably be better not to tempt the nausea by trying to hold it all together any longer. The tears burned my face. "I lost everything."

"Is that what happened? You turned into a monster and she just… what? Disappeared?"

Of course, he was trying to problem solve it: that's what he did. I knew that when I started blabbering like a damned idiot. I took a breath and tried to steady myself. He might be able to help if I could quit acting stupid long enough to give him the information he needed.

"I lost it when she called Šapat. Totally lost it. Scared the hell out of her. Beat the hell out of myself for it."

Nikolai nodded slowly. "When was this?"

"Um… week ago? Little more?"

"And then?"

I took as deep a breath as I could manage. "The overseers sent a hunter after me. Dumb kid came knockin' on the front door while we were eating lunch. She was gonna answer but I stopped her. Fuck, Nik, I grabbed her and it bruised her arm."

"Calm down, Alex." Nikolai patted my shoulder. "Just… just tell me all that happened."

"I… I didn't want to hurt the kid. I warned him off but… you know how they twist us." He was nodding. "I wanted… I was hoping… Belle would intervene. Get the kid out or me under control. Something. It didn't occur to me that… His first thought was that she was a prisoner. And the whole thing had her nervous because I was acting crazy. And her arm… fuck, Nik. Once the kid saw the bruise on her arm, it was over."

I heard him take a deep breath and then sigh. Unspoken-Nikolai for *would you quit cutting yourself off and just tell me what actually happened*?

"The kid got between us. Got her out of the house. Told me he'd be back for me." I took a deep breath. "He saved her. From me."

"Is that what he did?"

"Yes, Nik. That's what he did." Yeah, I was snippy. Wouldn't you be? "He got her the hell away from the monster that was fuckin terrorizing her."

"You left out the part about how I hung up on them."

As much as I desperately needed to hear her voice coming from behind me, I didn't dare trust it was real. Not the way my life runs.

"Because they may not have even sent the boy if I hadn't forced the issue that you could deny them."

I still couldn't bring myself to look in the direction of her voice. "*Belle*?" Of course, I didn't say 'Belle.' I said her name and Nikolai's eyes bugged almost completely out of his skull.

Then she was there, kneeling beside me and I was pretty sure the alcohol poisoning actually *had* killed me. "Forgive me, *cintaku.*" She leaned over and kissed me softly. "I had to save you from hurting him."

"But... how... I..." Yeah, coherent speech wasn't real high on my priority skill list right now.

"The boy insisted on returning me to my family." She really was there, beside me: explaining what had happened. I can't even begin to describe the relief. "So, I had him take me to the beach house."

"When Belle got out of a car we didn't recognize, calling for Mama and Papa, we knew something was wrong." Nikolai took over the story and I let the full reality that Belle was back at my side sink in. "So, we played along until the boy finally left and then Belle gave us the story. When we knew the boy was not watching either house, Belle and I came here."

Belle's arm was under my shoulder, helping me to sit up. The room didn't spin this time and there's no way you can convince me that it was only because a little more time had passed. My soul was back with me: my world was complete again. Now, I just needed to keep from fucking things up. Again.

"What are we going to do about the boy?"

I would have liked another couple moments to revel in the fact that I hadn't lost Belle, my mind, and my life in one shot but Nikolai was right: the kid was a hunter. He'd be back. And we needed to figure out how to safely beat him before I lost control and killed him. There were only a hundred problems, the most obvious ones being that we didn't have any clue what he was actually capable of or how much garbage the overseers had downloaded into his brain about me.

"Do we know anything about him at all?"

"He's called David." Of course, Belle knew about him. Duh. He'd rescued her from the evil monster: he had to talk to her and calm her down to get her to open up and give him someplace to take her. I knew how it worked. "He's seventeen and terrified of what it means to have been called."

Yet another reason I didn't want to tangle with the kid. Sometimes, the overseers called real arrogant little bastards: Billy Bad-Ass types without an ounce of common sense who were so wrapped up in being *chosen* that they don't bother being careful or smart. If what Belle said was true, though, this kid wasn't one of those: he was worse. He hated the calling but took it seriously.

Poor kid. I knew that feeling all too well.

"So, he'll be back." There was no question. I just needed to work through it out loud.

Belle nodded meekly. "I'm afraid so."

Now came the question I didn't really want to ask, mostly because the answer could really only confirm I was a hopeless drunk or an asshole rage-beast. Or both, I suppose. Not really helping but true. "How long was I out?" Belle looked absolutely terrified by the question. Tears started to form in her eyes. Great. "That long, huh?"

"We could not just rush over here, Alex. The boy was watching the house. Both houses."

"Damn it, Nik, I know the routine, okay? I just need to know how much time I've got to figure something out before he comes knockin again." As soon as I was able to shut my mouth, my head dropped. "I'm sorry. I..."

"You are an asshole. It is your nature. You are forgiven."

"Fuck you, Nik."

"It was almost forty-eight hours between the time he took me and the time you started to wake up."

I nodded. Not great news but not as bad as it could have been. "Then I've got a day... day and a half at most before the kid comes back to kill me." Of course, if I kept talking without thinking about how the words sounded, the look on Belle's face was going to kill me before the kid ever got a chance. "Which means I need your help, *nanm mwen*, to figure out how to keep both me and David alive without you here."

She looked stunned but, thankfully, Nikolai was already on the same page I was and spoke up before her expression completely destroyed me.

"Alex is right, you know. The boy has already saved you from the beast, no? If you are here when he returns, it is likely to cause additional complication."

She was still staring at me. Wounded.

"Baby, please." I took her hands and locked eyes with her. God, I needed her with me on this. "Help me figure out how to not kill this kid." I don't know if it was the tone of my voice or the desperation in my eyes and I'll probably never know: but whatever it was it got through to her and the little nod she gave was enough to give me hope that there was still some chance for me to not screw this up completely. "Help me control this."

The next eighteen or so hours was, hands-down, the worst supernatural training-montage sequence in existence. Between Nik puttering around the house trying to find the ingredients he needed and Belle trying to condition me to not lose control under duress, the whole thing felt like a waste. Just like that, though, the time was gone. Nikolai and Belle couldn't stay any longer or all the work we *had* been able to do would all have been for nothing.

I kissed Belle, told her I'd see her soon, and asked her to wait for Nik in the car.

"Take care of her." Nikolai nodded. He knew everything I was going to say as soon as I asked her to wait in the car, but he also knew I had to say it. "I'll call as soon as it's over. Give it a couple days before…"

"I come alone if it comes to that."

I nodded. We clasped hands. We embraced. It all felt so damned final.

"You will check in, yeah?"

I nodded again.

I watched Nikolai's beat-up old Jeep take off and disappear at the corner.

Now that they were gone and I could, hopefully, focus on what was ahead. I moved carefully through the house to prepare. I felt like I was working backwards: locking up my more dangerous weapons rather than readying them, moving those things that could improvise with deadly results out of the open areas rather than placing them in easy reach. It was weird, even difficult, to make my mind work that way but I had do what I could to make sure that I didn't hurt the kid.

While Nik and Belle were still here I had, of course, agreed with their stance that prep should be focused on neither of us getting hurt but now that they were safely en route back to the beach house I could deal with the reality of it.

I'd only had the one encounter with the kid but I knew him.

He was me all those years ago.

And short of a miracle, only one of us was going to leave this house.

If I had any say in the matter, it was gonna be him.

The house was as safe for him as I could make it. I glanced up at the clock on the mantle. If the kid had any sense, he was on his way here now: he'd have gathered his best weapons, added a couple new charms he never thought he'd ever use, and psyched himself up to come face me. To come kill me. I walked over to the bar and checked out what was left. Not much. I grabbed a bottle of Milagro and walked over and settled into my chair.

I'd spent a lot of my life actually wanting to die but now that I was sitting here waiting for it, I wasn't so sure. Once I'd figured out that the overseers were never going to let me go, I'd figured I would go out in a fight: but I'd never counted on being the monster. It was always going to be this way, though. One last fight with one hell of monster but, as it turned out, the only monster I was

going to be fighting was me and I was going to be fighting it to save the kid who
was coming to kill me. Or it. Hell, I don't even know anymore.

I pulled the cork and dropped it on the floor. No matter what happened
over the next couple hours, I wasn't going to need it again. I took a drink, then
another, then I leaned back and closed my eyes. "Come on, David." I checked the
time again. "Let's dance."

Twenty-three hours. On the dot. A car pulled into the driveway.

One car door: open then shut.

I'd left the front door unlocked. If he decided to come in that way it would
be easy and, without having to break into the house in broad daylight, he
wouldn't arouse the suspicion of the neighbors. Not that any of them really
cared for me much but it was always possible one of them might decide they
wouldn't wish a home-invasion on anyone: even me.

The front door opened then shut.

I took another drink.

He was moving through the house slowly. Safely. Careful to avoid the traps
he was sure I'd set for him.

"I'm in here, David."

I heard him stop. He was near the entrance to the living room but not quite
to where we could see each other yet. If I'd thought about it, I would have
turned my chair so it was facing away from the doorway. That would have made
it easier on him. He was inching toward the door. Now that he knew where I
was, he was even more concerned that I had set some sort of ambush. I didn't
blame him. I actually kinda admired his caution. Maybe they'd told him about
me after all. I mean… no matter what, I was always useful as a bad example.

"No tricks, kid." I took another drink. A long one. Might as well numb my
reflexes as much as possible while I was at it, right? "I'm unarmed."

He finally came around the wall: slowly, cautiously, his blade in his hand.
"How'd you know my name?"

"I know a lot of things."

He was keeping a lot of distance between us: sizing me up. Trying to figure
out the best attack, my defenses, and what was around that he or I could use if it
came down to it. Like I said: I know the drill.

"You know why I'm here, then."

"I know your mission." Christ, kid, it's not rocket science. "And I know
you're green. I know you're standing there right now trying to decide how many
weapons I'm hiding, how much of this bottle I've actually had to drink, and what
your chances of success are."

He looked like he wanted to argue then changed his mind. Either I was spot on or he was going to use it all against me later: I hadn't decided yet and, honestly, I'm not sure he had either.

"In order. I said I was unarmed and I basically am. I have no additional weapons hidden on or near me. I can't do anything about the natural ones, though." I took another long drink then held the bottle up, a little surprised that there was still about half of it left. "And this was full when I started."

"And my chances of success?" He seemed a little less cocky now, or at least a little less driven.

"That depends on if you plan to complete your mission or listen to reason."

And this is where I really hope the kid and me differ because it's right about the time when seventeen-year-old-me would have been flying across the room with the Ubojica headed straight for the monster's throat... and I was still at the point that I might forget to pull my counter-attack on the block (or be unable to) before it was too late.

"You're not like you were last time I was here."

"You're right about that, *chasè*." I took another drink. What the hell, right? We were either gonna talk or he was gonna kill me. "I gave myself alcohol poisoning after you left last time." Should I? Ah, hell... why not. "After you took Belle. And I know... I know she told you what you needed to hear but..." One more drink. "There's a lifetime of story there, too."

He took a couple careful steps toward me. "She gave me a pretty serious Beauty and the Beast vibe."

We were having a conversation. Thank God. Even with all I'd done to try to protect the kid from me, I didn't know what would happen if things went sideways.

"There's another chair." I pointed the mouth of the bottle toward the chair on the other side of the couch: close to the kitchen door and about as far away from me as you could get and still be in the living room. "If you want."

He took a hesitant step in that direction. "Why are you being so nice?"

"I don't wanna fight you, kid. I know you're young and strong and probably faster than me right now, but I don't even know what I'm capable of yet." I took another drink. The bottle was almost empty and, other than a little warmth in my throat, I really didn't feel anything. Not good for a number of reasons but I didn't have time to deal with them right now. "I'm okay with what you can do to me but I don't wanna do anything to you, so..."

He never put his knife away but he did sit down. It was a start. But what the hell was I going to do if I talked him out of killing me? What happened if the rage-beast clawed its way out and ended up hurting him? Or Belle? Or someone else?

"In fact, there's a part of me that's kinda hoping you *do* end up completing your mission. But I'd like for you to know why."

"Does it matter?"

"Not to me, man. But it might to you."

I could see the gears going in his head. "I'm listening."

I took another drink. The bottle was almost empty and I was really wishing I had another where I could easily get to it. Maybe, depending on how the kid reacted to everything, I'd get a chance to grab another one before he slit my throat.

"A couple months ago, I went to go deal with a *cauchemar.* You know what they are?"

He shook his head.

"Darkspawn. Otherworlders. Barely more predatory than scavengers. They pounce on your chest when you're asleep, usually in the middle of the night, and suck the life out of your lungs. If you're lucky, they break a rib when they hit you so the paramedics know to inflate your lungs." I looked at the bottle. Not even enough tequila left to make a decent margarita. I took another drink. There was one left: two if they were small. "Cliff's notes. I died. And when I woke up, I was different."

The kid nodded. "As one is when they wake up from being dead."

God help me, he's a smartass too. Could they have called one any more like me? Jesus!

"Little over a week ago, I went to deal with some hellhounds. You know what *they* are, right?" He was nodding. I wasn't completely sure he actually knew but he was getting bored with the back-story. At least, I would have been, so I assumed that was his problem. "The alpha and his pack took off when I told them to. Just took off." Another drink. Yeah. I set the empty bottle on the floor beside my chair. "Said I was in charge. The Otherworld Imperial here. And that's when I started to feel it."

"It?"

I nodded. I really wanted to go get another bottle but walking right past the kid to get to the bar didn't seem like the best idea at the moment. Of course, my whole perception of what was a good idea was in serious question anyway, so there was that. "The power. The rage. The beast." God, I needed a drink. "The beast you faced last time."

"Tell me something..."

"What's that?"

"Who is Belle to you? Really?"

"What do you mean?"

"She wasn't your prisoner, was she?"

"I don't think so." The kid was good. "But life shifted about fifteen degrees to the left real quick, so…"

"She wasn't being saved from you. She was saving you from this."

"She was saving *us* from this, kid, and the way things were going that day it's a damned good thing she did."

He nodded slowly. "You're an alcoholic, aren't you?"

"I'm just a drunk, kid."

"A drunk with an empty bottle. Looks uncomfortable." He leaned forward and set his blade on the table then nodded toward the bar. "Go ahead. I don't do sucker-punches or take cheap shots. Get what you need."

The overseers weren't usually dumb enough to call kids with compassion but I was kinda grateful they'd made that error this time around. I moved slowly: kept as much distance between us as possible for both our sakes… but I trusted his word and didn't try to watch over my shoulder or anything like that. If he was just letting me think I was getting through, maybe this would give him the edge when he went for the back-stab… but if we were actually having this conversation I didn't want to jeopardize it by being a suspicious prick. I grabbed a nearly full bottle of Jack Daniels and returned to my chair.

"You said Belle was saving both of us. What did you mean?"

Right back to it, then. Alright. "I'm just learning about this thing I am and I was having a really bad time of it. I still am. The monster's an asshole, man." I took a drink. "But I don't want to hurt you, kid. Hell, I *was* you. That's why I'm unarmed and trying to get myself a little impaired. So that if shit does *ale move*, you've got a better chance to kill me before I hurt you."

"Wait… What?" His confusion would have been funny if I were outside the conversation watching instead of sitting on the other side of it.

"I don't want to hurt you, David. I don't want to hurt anyone."

"And you're willing to die to..?"

"To keep from killing you?" I took a long drink then nodded.

"Who am I to you?"

"I told you, man. You're me. I *was* you. Young, strong, full of fire, out to save the innocent from the evil monsters that crept over from the Otherworlds."

"And now?"

I couldn't help it: I laughed. "Now, I *am* the monster and, honestly, I'm just too old for their shit."

"But I thought they only called…"

It took me a sec to figure out why he stopped but once I really looked at his face it was pretty obvious. Kid, someone should have warned you that I don't have enough feelings left to hurt. "Kids? Humans?" I took another drink. "Human kids?"

He gave me that little hesitant smile people give when you've just said the thing they were afraid would offend you if they'd said it. "I didn't mean…"

I chuckled. "Yeah, you did." Another drink. This poor kid couldn't figure out what he was supposed to be doing right now. But at least he wasn't attacking me yet. "And it's okay. Alright? I told you, kid: I don't wanna fight you." I leaned back in my chair. "I just wanna be that mean old asshole ex-cop that sits on their front porch and yells at the guys going thirty in a twenty-five, y'know?"

David smiled a little wider. "How's that workin out for you?"

If this cocky little bastard were any more like me, I'd be working on figuring out when they cloned me. And who *they* were, of course. "Well, your punk-ass is here so obviously I still got work to do."

He leaned forward and picked up his blade. This was it. I could almost hear his words before he even spoke.

"I don't wanna do this." He stood up. Yeah, this was it. "But I…"

"But you got your orders, man." I took another drink. "I get it. I do."

"I don't have a choice."

"I know." I took another drink then set the bottle down. "Dude, I really do get it." I leaned back in my chair and closed my eyes.

~19~

The house was quiet. It was dark but my vision was already adjusting. I closed my eyes before they even fully transitioned into whatever night vision being a monster gave me. My body ached all over and my hands were wet. Slick. It smelled like blood. The whole fucking house smelled like blood.

I'd closed my eyes too quickly to know exactly where I was but I was pretty sure it wasn't the living room. I stood up slowly, steadying myself on the carpeted floor. That narrowed down my location a little, at least.

I was weak. No. That didn't even begin. I was beat to hell. The kid was good, I had to give him that. Shit. Wait.

"Kid?"

Fuck. That wasn't my voice.

"Kid?! David?!"

I listened to the beast yell the young hunter's name and wanted to claw my own throat out just for making the sound. I needed to force my eyes open: to use the beast's ability to see in the dark to find the kid and help him. I was making a pretty bold assumption that he'd be in any shape to help but I had to do something.

I sucked in a deep breath and it was a hell of a lot harder than it should have been.

He broke a couple of my ribs. Good.

Open your eyes, you bastard. Either help the kid or face what you've done but open your fucking eyes.

It took a couple seconds but I finally managed to get my eyes open. They adjusted pretty much immediately to the darkness and I wished just as immediately that they hadn't. You know those so-called horror movies from the eighties where the only thing really scary about them is the amount of money they must have spent on fake blood? Well, that was pretty much the new interior design for my house: at least the living room and den. The furniture was broken and scattered and there was blood everywhere. The bar didn't even survive. Damned shame, that one: I could definitely drink myself into a coma right now.

I scanned the room again. There had to be something. Some sign.

Boots. Under the bookshelf. "Kid!" I crossed the room in what felt like two steps and heaved the shelf up off David's body. He moaned. Thank God. "David?"

He moaned again and his hand opened and felt around the floor beside him. Still looking for his blade. Damn, they picked a good one. "Don't move, man. I don't… I don't know what happened."

He coughed. There was so much blood I couldn't tell if the bit at the corner of his mouth was because of the cough or not. "You won, that's what."

"I definitely did not."

"It hurts, dude." He coughed again. Weaker this time. "Finish it."

"Come on, man. You're young and strong. Don't gimme that givin' up shit." I couldn't let this kid die. Not like this. There had to be a way to… the statue. I started looking. It had been on the shelf. It had to be right fuckin here. "Just hold on, kid."

"Why… why are you..?"

"Shut up, man." It had to be here. "Save your strength."

He was wheezing. Gasping. I could hear his fuckin heartbeat and it just kept getting slower. There! I scrambled across the floor and snatched up the mermaid statue. It hurt like hell to move like that but I didn't really care: besides, the statue was already doing its thing on me before I got it back to David.

I didn't know if it could handle both our injuries at the same time, but it didn't really matter. As much as I hated the thought of leaving Belle, I wasn't gonna let the kid die. Not if I could help him. I picked up his hand and wrapped it around the stone then sat back to let the magic do its thing.

I leaned back against the remains of my chair and wrapped my arms around my chest. One of those ribs the kid broke had shifted in my desperate scramble to get the statue in his hand. I closed my eyes, leaned back, and kept my mouth shut. If this was how it ended, I was okay with it.

For a second there, I felt like I was drowning then the rest of what was happening started to sink in. I felt the glass against my lips. The stone in the palm of my hand. It wasn't blood or water that was caught in my throat, it was bourbon. I swallowed slowly.

"Welcome back."

My vision was starting to clear but I couldn't believe what I was seeing. "Kid?"

David set his hand on my shoulder. "Don't try to move yet." He held the glass up to my lips again. "The bourbon was the only bottle not broken. Sorry if it's not your poison of choice for barely beating death, but..."

I chuckled. It hurt like hell.

"Didn't you have orders to kill me?"

"Will you shut up?" He pressed the glass against my lips. "You've got a ton of healing to do."

I sipped the bourbon and growled. "Answer the question, kid."

"Technically, my orders are to kill the monster that lives at this address."

I opened my hand and pulled it off the statue. I knew what happened to young hunters that didn't follow orders. "Get on with it."

David laughed and wrapped my fingers back around the stone. "Quit being so damned stubborn."

He kept his hand over mine so I couldn't drop the statue again. Fuckin punk. "Kid. I know who you get your orders from. I know how they work. Do what they sent you to do or they're gonna make your life hell."

"They sent me to kill a monster." Did he realize he was repeating himself? "Monsters don't save the lives of punk kids that break into their houses to try to kill them."

"Don't go gettin ideals, kid. They fuckin hate that."

We talked while the magic did its thing on me: talked about him, his school, the girl he was crushing on and we talked about me and Stefanie and Belle, talked about what it was like to be a hunter and what it was like to be hunted. After a while, when I was pretty sure neither of us were going to do anything too stupid, I leaned forward and took his hands.

"I need you to do two things for me, David."

"Sure, Mac. What do you need?"

"First, if you really believe it and only if you really believe it, check in and tell them you beat the monster."

Damn kid was already fishing his phone out of his pocket. "What's the other thing?"

"Bring Belle home."

"Sure thing, dude."

I kind of lost track of time sitting there but I knew better than to try to move too much. The mermaid statue simply wasn't enchanted to deal with this level of damage. I could still feel my ribs trying to piece themselves back together and if I jostled them around too much they'd end up healing in some weird shape that would kind of defeat the purpose of having the damned things. The kid was a hell of a fighter, I had to give him that. He'd seriously fucked me up while I was in full-on beast mode. The overseers knew exactly what they were doing when they called him to take care of me. Well... almost. They didn't plan on either of us having a conscience.

Of course, I had no way of knowing if he'd actually checked in mission complete or if he'd gone to bring Belle home or just to kill her since she was a monster, too. Hell, he could have been grabbing his phone to call in an airstrike. It didn't occur to me, until I was sitting here alone and basically helpless, just how much faith I'd put in the kid.

I guess if I was gonna pick a time to start trusting people, this was as good a time as any... or as deadly as any. Either way. Since I really wasn't the praying type, there wasn't much I could do but sit and wait.

I'm really not sure how long I sat there: long enough for my ribs to mostly heal correctly but not long enough for the pain to go away. It wasn't until I heard car doors that time even really meant much of anything at all. Two doors: opened then closed. Did the kid actually go get Belle and bring her home?

The front door opened and closed a couple seconds later. Two sets of footsteps. Thick soled boots and heavy steps. Whoever was in the house, it wasn't David and Belle. I took a deep breath and let it out slowly. I wasn't a hundred percent but I didn't have any more time to sit around waiting for a charm that was meant to heal magically-induced migraines, bruises and moderate gashes to put me back together again. I scanned the room as quickly as I could, looking for any weapons that might have been left scattered around after David and I fought. There wasn't much in easy reach but I could make do. I reached for one of the broken bottles on the floor and slumped against the broken end of the couch where I'd been leaning while I was waiting. I knew, now, what was in easy reach that I could use to fight whoever was coming up the hall. I just needed to know who I was facing and how much effort I was going to put into keeping the beast under control. Honestly, at this point, I didn't see much of a reason to worry about keeping the beast at bay: whoever was in my house wasn't someone I wanted there and, the way things had been going, I could only assume they were here for trouble.

I could hear them now: talking quietly to each other. They sounded like male voices: hushed and a little nervous. Wondering if I was still here: still alive. They called me by name so they knew who they were after... at least, they thought they did. Then, one of them went ahead and said the one thing either of them could have said that would have tipped the tables pretty much right on top of them.

"If that poor kid's still here, he's a corpse, but they want confirmation…"

The overseers had sent a clean-up crew to make sure David had done his job. Sent the kid after me then, as soon as he checked in, assumed the worst. Did they really think so little of his ability that they assumed I'd be able to pressure him into calling in mission complete? After calling someone who may as well have been me thirty years earlier, did they really expect him to cave? I hated the overseers now more than I had before, and that was no mean feat. I shook my head, closed my eyes and focused on that part of me that was keeping the beast under control then… I let go.

As soon as I let go of the beast, my senses went into overdrive. Not only could I hear them walking and talking, but I could hear the fabric of their pants brushing against itself and the creaking of the leather in their boots as they walked. I could smell them: leather, oil, exhaust, and fear. So much fear.

"McLaren?" I could hear it. The possibility that I might answer terrified him. "McLaren, you here?"

I stood up slowly. Silently. Rolled my shoulders and head just to get a feel for my body. This was going to hurt when it was over but it needed to be done. Well… I dunno… maybe it didn't need to be done… but I damned sure wanted to do it.

The first one came around the edge of the doorway.

I knew him.

Hell, I'd trained him.

"McLaren's dead."

"You don't look dead to me, Mac." His hand was closing around the hilt of his blade. Dumb move. "A little fucked up, maybe, but not dead."

"Is this the part where you add 'not yet' to your stupid little speech?"

"Come on, Mac." He took a step closer. "Don't make me do this."

"I told you, Carlin. McLaren's dead."

"Okay, I'll play." He took another step closer. What a fuckin idiot. I trained him better than that. "If Mac's dead, then who are you?"

I let the beast laugh. "I am *Segondè Kochma Wa* and you are uninvited in my home."

Carlin took another step and that put him in easy reach. Dumbass. "And what does all that mean?" Before I could answer, he lunged forward. Trying to catch me by surprise but all he did was unbalance himself. I swear I trained you better than that, you idiot.

I blocked his attack bare-handed except that, with the beast unleashed, my bare hand hit like a bowling ball with hay hooks attached for claws. "It means I'm your worst fuckin nightmare, Carlin, and you and your pal would be better off running."

He was cradling what was left of his arm but he'd backed out of easy reach. It was the first time since I heard them in the house that I cared one way or another what happened to either of them and I knew it wasn't going to last: but it was nice to care, if only in that fleeting moment.

"You know we can't do that, King Nightmare." The partner had come around the entry while Carlin stumbled backward. I didn't know him, but he knew at least enough about me to reach a decently accurate translation of the name I'd given them. Basically.

"I know you don't want to." I could smell it on him. This one was out for glory. He wanted his name on a plaque somewhere and he was too damned focused on that to realize that the only place his name would be displayed for generations was on his tombstone. "I know you're too hungry for glory to save your own skin." I took a step toward them. "So desperate to be remembered that you're willing to die today to achieve that shadow of immortality." I was swaying as I approached him. Stalking him and making damned sure he knew it. "You disgust me."

"You don't have to do this, Mac." Carlin, at least, had some sense of attachment to his future… at least in as much as he wanted one and had resigned himself to the fact that I was ready, willing, and able to take it away. "We were sent to check on the new kid and he's not here so…"

It was a valiant effort, sure, but ultimately futile. I knew how the overseers worked and they both knew I knew. If they'd been sent in that meant one of two things: either the council didn't believe David's mission report or they thought he was dead. The fact that they'd sent trained cleaners rather than a firebug meant they feared I was still alive and they wanted to make damned sure I was dead before they burned the house and salted the earth.

"Don't try to reason with it, Carlin." The other guy started moving forward. "I mean… look at it. That thing's not Alex McLaren. Not anymore."

At least he managed to get that part right.

His blade flashed as he dove toward me but, unlike with Carlin, I didn't feel anything that made me concerned for this guy or what kind of shape he'd be in after this was over. Carlin had been a friend, once: this guy wanted to make a name for himself by taking out the Big Bad and saving the world. Not today, dumb fuck. I hit his arm at the elbow and a thick wet snapping sound later he was one the floor writing in agony. Carlin was screaming at me, begging me to be merciful, but his voice sounded miles away and in my current state, that was probably a good thing. The more distance I perceived between Carlin and me, the more likely he was to be able to get away. I knelt beside the glory-hound, setting one knee on his shattered elbow, and leaned over him: my face in the air a little over a foot above his. He was trying not to scream, to hide his pain and fear even though he knew his death was literally just inches away. The smell of his fear and pain and pride all mixed together in that moment was like no high I'd ever experienced and the whole mix was actually making me drool. I was growling deep in my chest and gnashing my teeth while spit dripped off my lips onto his face. I could hear Carlin still begging me to show mercy but I couldn't… I couldn't stop.

I moved quicker than I knew I could and all the new guy's sounds of pain and fear muted into the bubbling gurgle that was coming from the place where his throat had been. I spit the flesh on the floor and licked the blood off my lips.

"Carlin." I didn't know how much longer I could keep from turning toward the other man. "Run."

I kept staring down at the man whose heart was still beating enough to pour even more blood onto the already soaked carpet. I heard Carlin scramble to his feet and heard his boots slamming against the wood floor in the hall. Car door. Car engine.

I laid my head down on the new guy's chest, only vaguely aware that the last gushes of blood from his shredded throat had soaked my hair.

After all my promises not to lose it. All my work to make sure I didn't kill the kid sent to kill me. All the soul-baring David and I had endured for him to be convinced I wasn't the monster they thought. After all that, here I was: laying on the still-warm corpse of a man whose throat I'd just torn out with my teeth: a man I didn't even know who, just like me so many years ago, was guilty only of trying to save the world.

Alex McLaren's brain was overwhelmed and disgusted and told me I should feel like I was gonna puke but that wasn't who was in charge. The barong ket didn't care about any of the promises I'd made to myself or if the corpse beneath me had deserved a chance to live or not. The only thing it did care about, apparently, was the fact that the Alex-brain was concerned because Belle would return soon and she would be heartbroken by what she found. I have no idea why the beast decided that Belle's opinion of things mattered but I didn't really care: as long as I was able to keep enough control not to do anything stupid.

Anything else stupid. Chewing this dumbass dude's throat out had been pretty damned stupid.

There was an engine on the street: speeding up as it neared the house instead of slowing. Tires chirped as it turned into the driveway and again as it stopped suddenly. Two doors. Open but not shut. It was David and Belle: and they knew something was wrong. I wondered what had alerted them: was there something outside? The front door still open? Had Carlin called the kid? The last one was unlikely: it's hard for most folks to work with a cell phone with a freshly broken arm.

"Mac?" The kid. He'd entered the house first: hopefully ready to fight whatever he ended up facing. He was a good hunter: he wouldn't barge in here after fighting me and not be ready for something. "Mac?!" There was a little more anxiety in his voice. Something in the hall had him worried. I heard Belle gasp softly. "Bud? You alright?"

"I'm alive but I'm not alright." Still wasn't my voice. Damn it. At least they had some warning about my state. "Slowly into the living room." I was pretty sure I had a handle on the beast but I didn't want to take any unnecessary risks. "Very slowly."

David's eyes opened a little wider when he came around the doorway but he managed to keep from displaying any intense reaction. I don't know if he thought the beast would jump on it or not: I don't remember anything that happened when the kid and I fought but I'd tried like hell to keep the beast out of that fight. Failed, of course. But I didn't even try this time. Hell, I took off the leash and gave it free reign. In retrospect, it's probably a miracle the new guy wasn't in a lot more pieces.

Belle came around the corner right behind David and showed none of his restraint. She rushed past the corpse and fell on her knees in front of me. "Oh, *cinta kerajaan ku*, are you hurt?"

"Physically undamaged, *nanm mwen*." Still not my voice. Shit. In spite of the probability that the beast was still very much in charge, her shoulders slumped a little in relief and I reached out and pulled her to me. "Forgive me for this."

She laid against my bloody chest and wrapped her arms around my waist. "It was necessary."

I wasn't sure I agreed but I couldn't argue. Not until I was fully myself, at any rate. The beast agreed with her assessment and was content to allow her touch to comfort me: I was just going to have to take what peace I could get.

"What happened, Mac?"

My eyes snapped up. I forgot the kid was still here. He jumped a little when my attention moved to him but not enough to make the beast pounce: at least not with Belle's arms around me. The possibility that Belle and my beast were dancing into Romeo and Juliet territory was an amusing tangent to consider but one that would have to be considered later. The kid was a hunter and a good one and he needed some answers.

"The overseers sent a clean-up team. Thought I'd killed you."

"No." David held up his phone. "I checked in mission complete."

I shook my head. It didn't make any sense. They didn't have the resources to send babysitters on every hunt. And if they did, knowing they'd sent someone after the person who'd literally written the tactical manual they downloaded into new recruits, why didn't they just send a team to begin with? The beast was getting restless. Angry. Nervous. Hungry.

"Help me, Belle."

"Mac?"

I shook my head. Alex McLaren was now simply a spectator whose last desperate play was asking the manticore for help. She responded to the request, of course, tightening her embrace and speaking words of love softly against my chest. The buzz of her voice against me was soothing but not quieting enough to let the boy off the hook.

"Who are you?"

"Mac... dude... I'm Dav..."

"Who *are* you?" The kid glanced desperately at Belle like he figured she was the only thing keeping him alive right now. He was right. "Really?"

The kid stuffed his phone back in his pocket. "Mac? What's goin on, dude?" He kept looking at Belle: watching her and my hands. He was moving slow and the kid was good but he wasn't that good. That brand-new shiny blade of his was going to take root in his chest if he made the move he was trying not to telegraph.

"You got one more chance to answer me, kid." Alex McLaren was somewhere in the back of my mind, begging me to give the kid time to explain himself. Belle was still pressed against me, trying to soothe my rage. Oddly enough, even though McLaren was depending on her to save the hunter, her voice never spoke of him.

"What do you want me to say, Mac?" His hand was moving toward his belt. Toward the blade. "You knew who I was and why I was here the minute I showed up."

My hands moved to Belle's shoulders as the kid drew his blade and she rolled away from me as he dove toward us. I grabbed his hand as the blade arced toward my neck. The kid was strong but nowhere near strong enough. I could see it, now: the same dedication to his original mission as the corpse on the floor. The same stupid drive: the same idiotic need to save the world from darkness. To save it from me.

"You're not stupid, kid." I squeezed his forearm until his fingers turned bright red. "Why are you doing this?"

He was in pain but he wasn't going to admit it. He answered me through clenched teeth. "How can you rip a guy's throat out and then ask me that?" He nodded toward the corpse but didn't move his eyes from mine. "Did you even hesitate?"

"Not as long as I have with you."

He chuckled: tried, and failed, to not sound like he was terrified to stand there looking death in the face. "Is that supposed to make me feel better?"

"Why else would you ask?"

He was struggling to free his arm, too dumb to admit it was a lost cause. Too dumb to admit that he'd already lost. His eyes darted to the side. "Belle? A little help?"

Interesting tactic. Did he actually think she was going to side with him?

I turned my head to look at her. "What say you, *hartaku*?" I wasn't sure what I'd do if she asked me to let him live, but Alex McLaren insisted I ask.

Belle lowered her eyes then bowed her head. "Your wishes define my desires, *cinta kerajaan ku.*"

I looked back at the hunter and smiled. He looked like I'd already ripped his guts out. "Got any other bright ideas, kid?"

It was fun watching his brain work: the fear and desperation overtaking his intelligence while he tried to come up with some way to keep his skin intact and all his internal organs internal. "Come on, Mac." God, the kid was desperate. "You wouldn't let this bastard kill me before."

"That's your hail mary?" I laughed, let go of his arm and shoved him backward. He stumbled and hit the wall as I rose to my feet. "Appealing to my human conscience?" I closed the distance between us easily and my hand closed around his throat. "Do you really think McLaren can save you?"

"C'mon, Mac." He was choking but continued to force himself to speak. "I know you're in there."

I couldn't tighten my fingers so I leaned forward, pressing his body against the wall and my hand deeper into his neck.

"Please, Mac."

There were tears in the kid's eyes. I wanted to laugh at him: to spit in his face and mock his plea… but I couldn't. My arm was shaking. I roared. This couldn't be happening. Belle's hand was on my arm: soft, gentle, pressing down. Moving my hand off the kid's throat. No! This couldn't be happening. But it is. You're losing. I'm back, bitch.

I pulled my arm clear of David completely and took a couple steps backward. "Belle, help him."

It was finally my voice that came out of my mouth.

I watched Belle help David slide down the wall to sit on the floor; watched him gasping for air as he eyed me suspiciously. I couldn't blame him. Hell, I'd have been worried if he *did* trust me right now. I still wasn't sure I trusted me right now.

I still didn't know how I'd managed to wrestle back control but my guess is that there were some magical safeguards set while Nikolai and Belle nursed me out of the booze coma after the first time David had showed up at the house. It was the only time they would have been able to set anything in place that the beast wouldn't know about. Whatever Belle was saying when I was holding her… when it was holding her… must have been the trigger.

"I'm sorry, kid." David looked over at me. "God, I'm so sorry."

"It wasn't you, Mac." His voice was raspy. Weak. He was in bad shape.

"What can I do?"

"Your mermaid." Belle didn't look at me. I couldn't blame her either. The barong ket triggered emotions written in her DNA that she couldn't handle and I had just let go of the leash and let it take total control. I wouldn't blame her if she patched up the kid, took him, and walked out.

I found the statue, walked over, and picked it up. I tried to wipe a blood smear off of it but it just made it worse. I looked around the room as I carried the little statue to Belle and David. "I can't guarantee the kitchen's any better, but the bedrooms might be a little less slasher-flick."

Belle actually looked up at me when I handed her the statue and let her hand linger on mine just long enough that I saw a glimmer of light at the end of a very dark tunnel. I backed away, though, as soon as she started to move the statue to David's hand. I stopped at the doorway and took a deep breath. I only had a few options right now and they ranged from bad-idea to really-fuckin-stupid: but I couldn't just stand there.

I walked through the kitchen to the basement door. I'd joked about making it a dungeon years ago, but Stefanie wouldn't let me put more than a thin little slide-lock high on the door to keep the little nieces and nephews from accidentally tumbling down the stairs. Now, I was really wishing I'd gone ahead and installed a real lock. Oh well. I pulled the door shut behind me and walked down the stairs in the dark. Not gonna lie: I was kinda hoping I'd trip and break my neck on the way down… or at least break enough bones that I couldn't hurt anyone for a while.

No such luck, of course. The beast may have been chained but its night vision was still a thing. I wondered how much more of its power I still had access to, but that was as far as it got: I wasn't going to push any limits without knowing what was actually going on with the whole situation. The last thing I wanted to do was undo whatever had been done to chain the bastard up.

I went to the corner furthest from the door and sat there, my legs folded in front of me and shoulders squared against the walls. Meditation seemed as good a way as any to pass the time: probably a better way than some of the other options that presented themselves when I was alone in the basement. When they were ready for me, Belle would figure out where I went: it wasn't really that difficult a conclusion to reach. My truck was still in the garage and I hadn't changed out of the blood-soaked clothes I was wearing: the odds of my walking down the street were pretty slim… and if I did, I'd get picked up by the cops in a heartbeat.

I just needed to sit here and wait.

~20~

My hand flew to the one touching my shoulder almost immediately.

It was thin. Soft.

"Mac?"

Belle. Oh God. I forced my fingers open and pulled my hand away.

"I'm sorry, *nanm mwen.* You startled me."

Belle smiled and kissed my face. "It's alright, *cintaku.*" It occurred to me, now, that there was light in the basement. The air smelled strongly of peroxide, ammonia, and Oxy-Clean. "But will you please go shower and let me wash those clothes?"

I looked down: everything I was wearing was caked with murky reddish-brown dried blood. My hands, my arms, my hair: all covered in it. I nodded slowly. "Belle, I..."

"Sshh." She stood up, smiled down at me, and held out her hand. "Come on. Up you get."

I took her hand and stood up. She started walking me toward the stairs.

"The kid?"

"He's fine." We stopped at the foot of the stairs. They weren't really wide enough for us to go up side-by-side, especially since I'd never gotten around to installing the handrail I kept meaning to. I motioned for her to go first so she did, then continued answering my question over her shoulder. "I called Nikolai once David was stable. He came over and did a thorough healing."

We were at the top of stairs and, thankfully, Belle seemed to have decided on natural light which wasn't quite as blinding.

"So, we won't see him again?" It seemed like a logical question. Considering the way his attempts to kill me had gone, I couldn't imagine the overseers sending him back here.

"Won't see who again?"

I blinked my eyes and shook my head. "No fuckin way."

David chuckled as he walked across the kitchen and handed me a beer. "You alright, dude?"

"What the hell are you doing here, kid?" I took a drink of beer and enjoyed the feel of the cold running down my throat. It was actually kind of intense.

"Shower." Belle pushed my shoulder gently. "Talk later."

"Yes, love." What else was I going to do? Argue?

I walked through the house, taking note of the very few things that weren't exactly as they were before. The blood was gone though and, honestly, I don't know how they managed it. One of the chairs was missing from the living room, probably too thoroughly destroyed to repair, and the bar was woefully understocked but, other than that… there was no evidence of the corpse, the bloodbath, or any of the other altercations before or after. I was almost able to ignore all that had happened.

Until I got to the bathroom.

The harsh fluorescent lights were unforgiving: forcing me to face every bloody inch of my body. I managed to get my shirt off but the way it landed on the floor, stiff from the dried blood, was too much. I turned away from the mirror and fell on my knees in front of the toilet and started to puke.

I have no idea how long I was in the bathroom. I puked up everything I'd ingested for a week, it seemed, then added about a half-gallon of stomach acid for good measure. When I finally managed to get in the shower, it seemed like an exercise in futility: the water washed the blood off in waves and every time I thought I was finally clean, there was more blood in the water. Always more blood. That could have been the title of my memoir: always more blood in the water. It's catchy, right?

Sometime while I was in the shower, Belle must have come in. When I finally started drying off, all the things I'd been wearing were gone and the room itself had been cleaned up some. There were clean clothes hanging on the hook behind the door.

I dressed, pulled my hair back in an elastic band, and went back to the kitchen.

David and Belle were sitting at the table drinking coffee like it was the most normal thing in the world.

"So… um… kid?"

"Have a seat, Mac." David chuckled and nodded to an empty chair.

Sure. Why not? Take the invitation of the kid sent to kill me, who I almost killed twice in return, to sit at my own kitchen table. Just in case my life wasn't fucked up enough, I guess. I shrugged and sat. "I kinda didn't expect you to hang around."

"Are you kidding me?"

"Um… no." Jesus Christ, I'd beaten this kid half to death, bit a guy's throat out, and then damned near choked this kid out. "I just figured that with all that's happened…"

"Mac. Dude. Chill. It's all good." I shook my head a little and Belle slid her coffee mug over in front of me. I picked it up and took a drink. I would rather have had whiskey, to be honest, but I wasn't going to complain about much right now. There was already too much weird shit to process to add anything else to my brain. "After Carlin's report, the overseers will be shitting themselves."

There was a vital piece of the puzzle that these two had and I didn't. "And why is this okay?"

"Because now they know, for sure, that you can take them out."

The kid sounded genuinely excited and pretty damned sure of the statement but I was already shaking my head. "Oh, hell no."

"But, Mac…"

"No, kid. Fuck. You saw what I did to Carlin's partner? What I almost did to you?" I set the coffee down and shook my head again. "I need a drink." I stood up and walked over to the cabinet where the couple bottles left in the kitchen were stored.

"But Mac…"

"No, kid." I pulled down a half-empty bottle of Jack and twisted off the top. "Listen to yourself for a second, huh?" I took a drink as I walked back across the room. "The overseers have survived this long by being ruthless. Do you know how they claw their way into your nervous system when they call you? The fuckers are carnage incarnate." I shook my head and took another drink. "They're not shittin themselves over anything."

David chuckled again and shook his head. "You don't get it, dude."

"You're right. I don't." I took another drink. "I'm telling you, kid, these guys are more than just a bunch of shitbirds with god complexes, okay? They've got power."

"Not over you, though."

I sighed. "Where did you hear a stupid thing like that?" I glanced over at Belle but she was shaking her head.

"Come on, dude. As soon as you hung up on them, they went ballistic." The kid was way too excited about the news he was sharing. "They started calling people in left and right. Looking for the perfect balance of hunters to send that would be able to get to you before you came for them."

"Coming for them was never on my radar, kid." I took another drink. "I just wanted them to leave me the fuck alone."

"Well, whatever vibe you sent them, what they read was that you were gonna tear them apart."

I analyzed the bottle in my hand just to keep from looking at either of the people I was sitting with. If the kid was right, this was a damned nightmare. "How'd you end up on the strike team?"

"What?"

I looked at David, locked his eyes with mine, and repeated myself. "How... did *you*... end up on the strike team?"

"Pelledna put me on point because he said I'd remind you of yourself."

I nodded. "Well, the fucker was right about that." I took a drink then set the bottle down. It was almost empty anyway. "So why are we sitting here now? Having this discussion?"

"You tell me, Mac. They sent me in a dead man. Figured I'd be the martyr that would galvanize the rest of the team to do what needed to be done."

God, I hated those bastards. "Sent you in to be their martyr." I was nodding. The more David talked, the more I was considering making the insane suggestion that I was targeting the overseers a reality. "To make sure everyone hated me for killing a seventeen-year-old kid."

"That was their plan."

Belle's hand rested lightly on my arm and I turned my attention toward her. "You beat them, *cintaku*. Twice. First when you denied them control and second when you kept the barong ket from killing David." She flashed that little mischievous smile that drives me absolutely crazy. "They're right to be afraid of you, Mac."

"I'm tired, Belle." I shook my head and squeezed her hand gently. "I just want to be left alone, but..." I wasn't going to finish it. I didn't have to. Both Belle and David knew the rest of the sentence.

"I'm with you, Mac." David nodded sharply. "We had a hell of a fight but I know the only reason I had any chance at all was because you let me have one. It's simple. At least to me. They sent me on a suicide mission. You saved my life. They have their claws in me now, but you have my loyalty."

"If we're gonna do this, we're gonna have to be smart about it." Right. Be smart about the stupidest of stupid ideas I'd entertained in a very long time. "We're gonna have to seriously prepare. Find all the big guns we can. Train until everything is second nature. It's not gonna be easy." The kid was eating it up. I can't tell who's the bigger asshole right now: the overseers for sending the kid in as cannon fodder or me for pumping him up to fight back. "Kid, think about this. What about your aunt? And that girl... What's her name? Gina?" Come on, David, change your mind.

"How can you even ask me that, Mac?" The kid was passionate. Animated. "It's supposed to be my sacred duty or some shit to save the world from monsters, right?" He slammed his fist on the table and I tried not to smile. "Those assholes are the biggest monsters out there right now!" I told him not to go getting ideals but apparently the kid follows orders about as well as I do. Go figure.

Belle laughed softly. "God, he sounds familiar."

"Not helping, *nanm mwen.*"

David smiled.

Yeah, *definitely* not helping.

"Will you at least *talk* to your aunt before you decide you're all in on this?"

"And tell her what, Mac?" David leaned back in his chair and held his hands up, waiting for me to tell him something. Anything. And I had nothing. "That the world is full of monsters and I'm part of the solution? That there's a war coming and I'm signing up for the first wave? Come *on*, Mac!" He shook his head and scrunched his face up a little. "What part of that conversation is gonna end well?"

Belle leaned over and set her head on my shoulder. "He's older than you were, Alex. *Biarkan dia memutuskan.*"

I sighed. She was right, of course. He was a lot older than I had been and no one had second-guessed me or tried to talk me out of doing what needed to be done. And the only argument I could come up with was that there was that there hadn't been anyone like me around to force me to reconsider. Ultimately, though, it was the kid's decision and I had to let him make it. Whether I liked it or not.

"This could be a suicide run, kid. You understand that, right?"

David nodded. "And unlike the last one, I know that going in and I've got the option to bail on it."

"Yes, you do." I nodded. "And, honestly, there's part of me that wishes you would bail on it."

"And the other part?"

"The other part..." God damn it, kid. If I say it, it's a done deal and we all know it. If I don't say it, he's gonna drag it out of me and Belle will probably fuckin help him. "The other part can't think of anyone else I'd rather have on my wing for this shitshow."

"Where do we start?"

Even at my most idealistic, I wasn't this gung-ho. At least, I don't remember being this gung-ho. I'm pretty sure that, if I were to ask, I'd get told otherwise. Yeah - this is me not asking. "The liquor store."

"Seriously, Mac."

"Oh, I'm serious, kid." I leaned back in my chair and nodded slowly. "We flat-out trashed the bar and if we're gonna do this, I'm gonna need a hell of a lot more booze than we've got in this house right now." David started to smirk but I guess the fact that neither Belle nor I had even cracked a smile changed his mind.

"Okay, then."

~21~

The first couple days were a blur of activity.

I knew the kid and I were going to have to work up some new tactics to face the overseers as a team. They didn't train us to work that way: everything they downloaded into the next *chosen* was designed to work as a one-person show.

The physical stuff was easy enough to adapt. Just a bunch of repetitive sparring to make sure we were in sync with whatever had to happen. Daily repetitive boring ass practice.

It was nice to have something that didn't require too much work.

Remember when I said I was a shit witch? That I knew a bunch of shit but it just wouldn't work?

So, we're out in the backyard (which has some kind of magical shielding that would make nosy neighbors see me and David playing catch or some stupid shit) and David's having a hard time getting this one simple spell to work.

"Focus on your target. We've already done the ground work." I feel like a fucking idiot trying to teach him something I can't do but that's where we are. "Use your hands to target if you need to." I waited for him to catch up. "Then… *auferetur.*"

And, as expected, the target kinda shimmied a little but didn't bother actually moving away.

David laughed. "Great job there, Mac."

"Yeah, well, magic's not my thing."

Belle shook her head. "Do something for me, Mac?"

"Anything, *namn mwen.*"

She smirked. "Try it like I would."

I sighed and shook my head. We'd been through this hundreds of times: trying different types of magic to see if I could manage to do… well… anything. Nothing had ever worked. But… Belle asked and I did agree. Some day I'll remember to find out what I'm agreeing to before I agree.

My heart wasn't in it. It was a stupid waste of time. I lifted my hand, palm facing the target, and grumbled. "*Tolaivil.*"

Belle giggled softly and both mine and David's mouths dropped open as the target slid several feet away from us.

"What the hell?"

"You weren't fully human before," Belle said, explaining her theory excitedly. "That's why you could never get human magic to work."

"And I wasn't fully an otherworlder either…"

"Do you know what this means, *cintaku?*"

"That I've got more homework," I grumbled. David and Belle both laughed but I really didn't feel like wasting a bunch of time trying to learn the whole scope of magic again. Maybe after. "Just give me the basics, *namn mwen.* And you…" I shook my head at David. "You hiding some otherworld blood, too? Because you're not doing a hell of a lot better than I ever did."

"I don't think so." At least the kid was taking it seriously. He sighed and looked over at the target. "I mean… it would be so much easier if I could just…" He lifted his hand and flicked his fingers like he was thumping a fly off some imaginary thing in front of him and the target slid back another foot.

"What the fuck?" I wasn't sure at first which one of us said it but I decided it must have been both.

"And the boy's a natural," Belle said with a smile. "The council doesn't stand a chance."

There was only a split second between Belle's statement and what happened next but David and I had established a rhythm to our practice that made our next move almost automatic: we both turned toward the target and cast the spell to push it away.

The target didn't move, though, and David and I flew apart like a couple of high-powered magnets when you try to force the same polarities together.

I rolled out of the landing and checked quickly to make sure David had been able to do the same. I expected some sage amusement from Belle explaining what we'd done wrong, but her face was just beginning to soften from the panic that took over when we both went flying.

"Are you two alright?"

"God damn, that was pleasant," I grumbled as David and I both walked back toward where Belle was standing. "You okay, kid?"

David was rubbing his shoulder and nodding. "What the fuck was that?"

The only theory we could come up with was that the powers were in conflict but that didn't make sense to me. I mean, they could coexist easily enough: hell, Nikolai and Coralia had been using their magic side-by-side for a couple hundred years.

"*Ah, but we do not work together, otprysk*" Nikolai explained over the phone. "*We can compliment each other's work but the forces will not cooperate. At their deepest levels, they were made to make war on each other. You understand?*" I didn't. "*You notice that when Coralia shields you I do not, yes?*" I'd noticed but never really thought anything about it. "*We both agreed that it was better to have only one do that work than to have the work canceled because the forces were in conflict. It is a delicate balance, Alex. You understand?*"

Yeah. I understood. I understood that the kid and I had more work ahead of us than either of us had bargained for.

We had problems to face, though, and the biggest one, as far as I was concerned, was that there was no way to tell when the overseers would strike again. Considering what I'd done to the other guy and the probable content of Carlin's report, we could assume they'd written the kid off as a loss. At least, they hadn't rolled down any new missions to him: whether it was because they thought he was dead or compromised was unclear but, either way, we were free to prepare. Good thing, too. We needed all the prep time we could get.

Because the second biggest problem was that the kid had never fired a gun in his life.

I know, I know… you can't use a gun against otherworlders, right? The only way to really vanquish them is with magic and enchanted weapons and shit, right? Trust me… I've heard it all and, to some extent, it's true. In order to actually win the fight, you do need those things… but never underestimate the upper hand a surprise shot from a nine-mil can give you. Especially against a being that's not expecting you to use a gun.

Luckily, the kid was as quick a study on the range as he was everywhere else.

The more we trained, the more optimistic I got about the possibility of victory and that was always a dangerous situation. If there was one thing I'd learned over way too many years of fighting this fight, it was that feeling good about the upcoming battle was a sign that something catastrophically bad was gonna happen.

So here I was, waiting for the overseers' other shoe to drop. Again.

It didn't take nearly as long as I'd hoped.

It had been a brutal day: up before dawn and training every moment. Seriously, the only thing that could even be considered a break was the ten-minute trips to and from the range. We were so close to ready.

Belle had just yelled down the basement stairs that dinner was ready and David and I were on our way up. The mundane normalcy of it was palpable.

I should have known something was gonna happen.

David was almost to the top of the stairs when it hit.

He didn't even have to say anything: I already knew what I was seeing. I grabbed him as he started to fall and eased him up the last couple stairs to the kitchen floor.

"Belle! Find his phone!"

I sat beside David and set my hand on his shoulder. "I know, kid. It feels like your drowning in your own blood. Spike through your head."

He nodded and opened his mouth like he wanted to say something but couldn't.

"They're activating you for a mission."

He shook his head weakly.

"Yeah. I don't think you get that option, kid."

Belle returned with his phone just as it started to ring.

"You gotta pick it up, man."

David held his hand out and Belle set the phone in his palm. It rang again and I could see the defiance flash in his eyes.

"Answer the call, son."

He closed his eyes and swiped his thumb across the screen as he set the phone next to his ear.

Somewhere in some little side-room in my mind, it occurred to me that I'd never experienced a call from this perspective. I could describe, in excruciating detail, what David was enduring but now, for the first time, I was seeing it from Belle's and Stef's and Nikolai's point of view… and I gotta tell you: the utter helplessness while you sit by and watch someone you care for get told to go fight to the death… it sucks.

David's eyes glazed over and his body finally stopped trembling. The download was starting: all the information the overseers thought he'd need to fight whatever it was they were sending him after being transferred directly into his brain. It was actually a damned efficient system… it was just that the assholes that employed it had lost what little humanity they'd retained over the centuries and their decisions were reflecting that.

That was why it was time to take them out.

Now, though, it would have to wait until David's mission was complete. Whatever it was.

"Does it always take this long?"

Belle set her hand on my shoulder. "Yes, *cintaku*." She kissed my face softly. "Every time."

Another one of those side-rooms in my brain started making a note… no, etching in stone… that my greatest strength had pretty much nothing to do with me. How many times had Stef and Nik and Belle sat through this torture just to watch me leave a few hours later knowing I might not come back?

Oh God. What if he lost the fight they were sending him into? What if the kid didn't come back?

Stefanie had said, once, that the Universe must have really hated her since it decided the love of her life couldn't give her children. She only said it once because she knew how much I wanted to give her everything she ever wanted. Now, though: sitting here waiting for the call to disconnect, I wonder if it wasn't actually the Universe casting a rare glimmer of mercy in her direction. And mine.

David pulled the phone away from his ear and swiped the screen to disconnect the call.

"Kid? You okay?"

David shook his head.

"What? What did they send you?"

He shook his head again. "We're out of time, Mac."

"Nah, kid." How the hell did Belle do this? "We got time. You just gotta kick this one out and…"

"No, Mac." I knew the look on his face and it was way down the list of ones I wanted to see. "We gotta move on them. Now."

"Who's your target, kid?"

David closed his eyes and shook his head. There were tears forcing their way out from under his eyelids. The realization was like a bowling ball to the gut. I felt Belle's lips on my cheek: heard her whisper that I would know where to find her when it was safe. Then she was gone.

"Alright, kid." David looked up. The anguish on his face over having been ordered to kill Belle broke my heart. More than that, though, it did something I didn't think was possible. The order to kill Belle stoked flames of a rage I hadn't even realized existed: flames so deep and cold that I knew they'd never escape it. I was pretty sure there was no way I could have been any more angry… until I saw the kid's face and knew he was just as angry as I was. "Let's end this."

Three hours later, David and I were in my truck on our way to the beach house.

While we were both pretty good with the magic we'd learned and been practicing, it never hurt to have a little extra firepower up your sleeve.

Nikolai was more serious than I'd seen him in a long time and, considering the way things had gone recently, that was a pretty serious statement.

"I have to counsel against this course *otprysk.* You know that, right?"

"I know, Nik." Of course, he had to. He'd sent me on enough suicide missions and now I was dragging a kid along with me on one. "But you're not changing my mind and while..."

"Or mine."

I shrugged. I was gonna say something about not speaking for the kid but David went ahead and made that a non-issue.

Nikolai nodded slowly. "Very well, then. Come."

He led us back to the workroom. The table was neat and orderly and I somehow managed to resist making any cracks about it. Orderly rows of trinkets: pendants, rings, little figurines similar to the paladin I'd given the kid my nemesis attacked. Nikolai pointed at the table. "David, you choose here. If you need help identifying them, you ask, huh?"

That was a jab at me and I knew it but I let it go. It seemed like a lifetime ago, after all, when I'd grabbed a bunch of trinkets I guessed would be useful with pretty dismally terrible results.

"*Otprysk.*" Nikolai had moved to another table and pointed down at it. "Your charms are here."

It took a split second for my brain to catch up. I nodded as I joined him at the table.

"Did Coralia..."

"She's less happy to assist you on this *komandirovka*[11] than I am. Best not to speak of it to her until you come back, huh?"

Subtle, old man. Real subtle.

"You set, kid?"

David looked over from the table and nodded. I couldn't tell at a glance what all he'd grabbed but I did notice he'd snagged at least a couple things I would have suggested if he'd asked.

---

[11] mission

Nikolai clasped my hand. "You come home, *otprysk,* and you bring that boy with you."

"I will, Nik." Why did all our goodbyes lately feel so damned final?

Back in the truck, with the beach house in the rearview, David asked one of the questions I'd been waiting for: one I was actually sort of in a position to answer.

"So, what's the deal with you and the witch?"

I laughed. "The deal with me and the witch?" I said I was in a position to answer, but that didn't mean the kid wasn't gonna have to work for it. "You're gonna have to be a little more specific, kid."

David laughed a little too. "Okay. I mean… it's obvious you guys've got some pretty serious history. How far back do you go? And what's that thing he calls you?"

I guess he figured it was important to have a decent understanding of the guy whose magic he just loaded up with. Not a bad idea, really.

"I've known Nik and Coralia almost thirty years, I guess." It didn't seem possible, but the math worked out. "Before the whole barong ket thing, I was a pretty shit witch. Nik heard about my failures with magic and reached out." Way oversimplified, but it worked.

"And that thing he calls you? Obrisk?"

Oh hell. "I dunno. It's just a thing he calls me." Yeah, I lied. Sue me. Now was definitely not the time to tell the kid that Nik was basically just calling me his kid. The same way I'd basically started calling David the same damned thing. Weird-ass uninvited parental-type emotion and all. Son of a bitch. It wasn't the time for either of us to have to deal with it.

"Uh huh."

"What?"

"You really expect me to believe a witch has called you the same thing for almost thirty years and you never asked what it meant?"

Jesus Christ. "It means… like… kid… or something."

David smirked and nodded but didn't say anything else. This was gonna be a really weird conversation later… assuming we got out of this, that is. Right now, as I parked across the street from the unassuming little office complex where I knew the overseers were hidden, the outcome was still anybody's guess.

At least I didn't feel confident anymore.

"This is it?"

"You don't sound too impressed."

David looked out the windshield at the complex and shrugged. "I guess I expected something a little more... I dunno... more."

I couldn't help but chuckle. The first time I tracked this place down, I had the same reaction. "You ready for this, kid?"

David's face lost almost all emotion. I knew the look. "If you'd asked me yesterday, I might have still been unsure." Yup. That was the look. The call targeting Belle had decided it.

"Then let's do it."

~22~

We walked through the door into the office that hid the entrance to the overseers' lair. The door said it was a consulting firm, but there wasn't a soul in the city that could tell you who consulted with them or about what. The woman behind the desk looked up when the door opened and looked back down almost immediately. She'd been here the last couple times I'd come and we had an understanding: I knew she was a gatekeeper not a receptionist and she knew that when my shadow darkened that door it meant bad shit was about to happen.

She'd done whatever she thought she needed to do in preparation to face me and stood up, shaking her head as I started walking toward the door that lead to the inner part of the office. "McLaren, you're…"

"Oh, they're expecting me."

"You know I have to…"

"Don't." I spun quicker than I expected. The beast was ready to take over and I was damned near ready to let it. The gatekeeper jumped but David, who'd already dealt with the asshole beside him more than anyone should have to, didn't even blink. Honestly, I kinda loved the fact that the kid wasn't fazed… but it didn't do much for the gatekeeper's resolve. She raised her hands about halfway up her torso, palms out, and sat back down.

I looked over at David and felt a wave of guilt. There was no sending him away now: no saving him from the apocalypse we were walking toward. I felt one last wave of guilt and fear, knowing that once the shit truly hit the fan anything could happen… then I let the beast push it out of my head: I couldn't let my concern for him dull my ability to watch his back.

I pushed open the door to the conference room.

Near the head of the table, four men stood looking down at the table like they were examining some business proposal… except that there was nothing on the table. Behind them, the polished presentation wall sparkled under the blinding LED light fixtures.

"Gentlemen, give us the room."

The one nearest us looked up and laughed. "You're one arrogant son of bitch, McLaren."

I smiled and rolled my shoulders. The gatekeepers had always been annoying but there was a distinct difference today.

Today, they were serious.

And I didn't give a fuck about any of them.

All four faltered when I turned toward them but the one that spoke went flying backward before I could even react.

"Watch your mouth, asshole."

Apparently, the kid decided we were in it.

Who was I to argue?

The next one started to move and I lunged toward him. I wrapped my arms around his chest and used his momentum to spin him around and toss him none-too-gently on the conference table. He landed with a thud, followed with a weak moan.

The other two started to move around the edge of the table and David and I squared our shoulders to create a barrier between them and the door.

"You can't win, McLaren. You know that, right?"

I hadn't realized I knew any of the guys in the room when we walked in but I recognized this one now. Edgar Pelledna. The one that sent David in first because he knew the kid would remind me of myself.

"Not sure how you figure that, Pelledna." I was swaying again. Stalking him. And I hadn't even bothered to let the beast move in. Guess it was gonna be like that, this time. "Considering you're pretty high on my hit-list."

Pelledna hesitated before he took his next step and the beast took that split second to close the space between us completely. I was inches from him, growling softly in his face.

"Now, McLaren… let me expla…"

"No."

I could smell the fear he was trying to hide and all it was doing was pissing me off even more.

"We had to…"

My hand was around his neck. "You sent the kid to kill me knowing he'd fail." I was squeezing. Pelledna's face was starting to turn red. "Hoping that he'd get a couple decent shots in first because I'd see myself standing there." It wasn't a question so the fact that Pelledna was trying to shake his head meant pretty much jack shit.

Beside me, the other guy had lunged for David but the kid was better and faster than the idiot that attacked him. I didn't have to worry about what was going on there.

"Mac… please…"

"How the fuck can you still make noise?" I snapped, squeezing even harder. "You fucked up, Pelledna." I leaned closer: close enough to whisper in his ear. "You sent me the son I could never have, Pelledna. You sent me all the reason I need to finish this."

I let Edgar Pelledna fall in a heap on the floor, not really caring what kind of condition he was in, and turned toward David. The kid was on his feet, standing over the unconscious body of the guy who'd attacked him.

"You okay?"

"Yeah."

I turned to face the wall the gatekeepers had failed to protect, David moving smoothly to my side. The wall looked like one of those huge dry erase boards people install in places like this so they can show their slides and write all over the place then have the janitors wipe it all away later.

I'm sure it worked that way, too.

And when I'd been here before, I'd gone through the hassle of using the spells that properly opened the damned thing and alerted everything on the other side that they were about to have company.

There were a couple major differences this time around, though.

For one thing: the other times I'd been here, I was human… or thought I was. Something about the whole process had seemed necessary.

Another thing: those other times, I'd just been there to talk.

David looked at the wall then at me. "Mac?"

I was still there. Sort of. But only barely. "Pretty much nope."

He smirked and nodded sharply. "Your highness."

"You ready?"

He nodded again.

I drew my pistol. "Watch your eyes, kid." Then fired dead-center of the shimmering wall.

I've never shot a whiteboard before but if, when you do, it shatters into a bunch of long white pieces of shrapnel then I guess it actually was a giant whiteboard.

Was.

I walked toward the passage that had been hidden by the whiteboard. I didn't even have to check to see if David was with me. I could feel him beside me: he was angry enough that the rage he was holding was actually raising his body temperature and elevating his heartbeat. I could smell the adrenaline already working its way through him. I wasn't too keen on agreeing with the beast on anything, but even it agreed that I couldn't have had a better second on this one.

We walked down the roughhewn corridor: chiseled from black stone that actually existed thousands of miles and another dimension away from the entrance I'd just destroyed. The overseers hid as far away from the chaos they instigated as possible and, while it had kept them safe for centuries, their time was up.

It occurred to me as we walked that I'd never wondered, before, just how many dimensions we were about to pass through or what impact that travel might have on the kid. I'd made this journey a few times when I thought I was human but I wasn't. Not completely, anyway.

"You okay, kid?" My voice was gone, buried completely under the beast's, and it was weird to hear the deep growl verbalizing the concern I was pretty sure was a hundred percent mine.

"Is it okay to be angry?"

I wanted to hug the kid and send him away, but instead I just nodded and grunted a sort of affirmative response to his question.

"Then I'm okay."

We walked a little further. "There are four gates," I told him as we continued on our journey. "The first was the one in the office. We'll be at the next one soon."

I didn't know how I knew: I'd honestly never paid attention to how long it took to get from one gate to the next. But I could feel it. More accurately, I could feel the resistance of the next set of gatekeepers building as they received word that we were headed their direction.

"I want to destroy them all, but..."

"Don't do anything you can't live with, kid." Leave that shit to me. I'm already dead. "Don't let them do that to you."

He didn't answer and we kept walking: I could only hope he'd actually processed what I said, and maybe even the shit I didn't say, and was using that advice to temper whatever he was going to do next.

Because we were at the next gate and out of time.

They came at us from four different directions: compass points, the beast told me. Closing on us slowly: banking on the shock-value their half-rotted appearance should have instilled... but they either underestimated Hollywood's ability to desensitize folks to the walking dead or they just underestimated us: not sure which. Not that it mattered.

"Tolaivil." The beast's growl made the spell sound a hell of a lot scarier than it actually was but the spell worked, which was all that really mattered. All four flew backward. Beside me, David closed his fists and they stopped: frozen and suspended in mid-air.

I chuckled and patted David's shoulder, trying to ignore the claws that were forming at the ends of my fingers. "Good one."

I punched the door in our way: a once solid wooden thing that seemed to have been rotting along with its guards. It splintered and we kept walking. I still had decent control of the back of my brain: enough to try to convince myself that the door really had been falling apart before I shattered it with one hit... enough to try to convince myself that literally obliterating the gates between these dimensions wasn't opening up a much bigger can of worms than David and I were prepared for...

The beast's consciousness, though, wanted the Alex-brain to quit trying to justify everything and let it take care of doing what needed to be done.

"Are *you* alright?"

It took a second to wrap my brain around the fact that the kid was asking me that... that he was apparently concerned about me. I knew I was concerned about him and taking him into this mess but it actually had never occurred to me that he might give a shit about what happened to me during all this. "Fine." Yeah, I lied. It happens. Last thing I needed was for the kid to get sloppy because he was worried about me.

"Two down," I told him as we walked side-by-side down the black corridor. "They could be mounting major resistance at the next one, considering..." I shrugged. "Considering. But they don't have a hell of a lot of resources between here and the chamber. We've already cut them off from their best options for reinforcements."

"If you know so much about them, why didn't you do this before?"

It was a valid question. If I had done this before, he wouldn't be here. He wouldn't have ever known about this shit.

He could have been a normal kid.

When I thought I was human, I'd been afraid of them: terrified of what they could do and the carelessness with which they did it. The only thing that mattered, then, was keeping what precious few things I held dear safe… and that meant not rocking their boat. I could have said that, and the kid probably would have been okay with it all, but instead I answered "I was an idiot."

David laughed. "That's all you got, huh?"

I shrugged and we kept walking. It definitely wasn't all, but I wasn't going to get into it now: not while we were heading toward the next gate… heading toward the council. It was either going to end in freedom or death for both of us: it really wasn't the time to dwell on the whole *what would I do if I could do it all again* bullshit.

Not that the beast would have allowed it. Not right now, anyway.

The hall widened and a tall metal gate and a half-dozen armed guards that looked like centaurs made with snakes instead of horses.

"What the hell?"

"Naga," I answered.

They were moving toward us and David faltered. "You okay?"

"I hate snakes," he replied.

The beast laughed. "Use it, son."

I don't know what I expected to happen but David nodded sharply and squared his shoulders beside me. I hated the beast in that moment for being the one that gave David the strength to stand at my side… but I also kinda loved the fact that it knew what to say to give the kid the boost he needed.

I drew the Ubojica. "Don't try to cast, son. They'll raptor strike our asses as soon as we're wrapped in the spell." Why the fuck did I keep calling him *son*? God damn it.

David nodded and drew his blade. "Old school it is."

I shook my head as we moved so our shoulders made a v-shape that pointed at the gate: the naga were advancing slowly but they were still advancing. It wasn't a conscious thing, but I started to growl as they neared and the pair closest to us pulled back.

"What's wrong?" The beast was enjoying it and, honestly, so was I. "Were you expecting someone else?"

"You've changed, McLaren."

Way to state the obvious, cobra commander. "And?"

"You were not sssummoned."

"No shit." The way they dragged out their eses had been unnerving the last time I'd faced them but this time it just annoyed me. "But we're here." I rolled my shoulders and smiled. "And we're going through that gate."

"You misssssunderssstand…"

I growled, hoping the kid would pick up on the vibe that shit was about to go down.

"Your admisssssion iss not sssanctioned by…"

The beast was bored and I was irritated. I dove toward the commander and the Ubojica sparkled in the cavern's unnatural light. "I didn't ask, deathnoodle." My blade sunk deep in his shoulder, making him drop his spear. "I didn't ask them and I'm not asking you."

His buddy moved on David but the kid took the beast's advice and used the fact that his opponent was half snake to his full advantage. The naga was quick, but part of being half snake made them depend on being able to intimidate their prey and the kid took that away. The naga's intimidation attempts ended up telegraphing every attack it made and the kid was taking it down with ease.

The next pair started to move in as I drew my blade across the commander's throat but the last two held their positions: waiting for us to make a mistake so they could swoop in from the flank and tear us up.

It would have been a great tactic, too… if we'd been unaware of it and had actually made the mistakes they were expecting us to. We'd hit that point, though, where it was all a dance and David and I were the best pair on the floor. All the training was paying off.

We made quick work of the second pair and turned, simultaneously, toward the remaining naga.

"Open the gate."

I wasn't even surprised that David had beat me to the demand.

The one nearest the chain that pulled the gate open turned away from us and began to pull on the chain in spite of its partner's demands not to. As we started to walk through the gate, the one that still thought it wanted to stop us advanced. I snapped toward it and growled as we walked by which was, apparently, enough to make it rethink its dedication.

David chuckled as we walked away from the gate.

"What's so funny?"

"You give like zero fucks about anything right now, don't you?"

My brain kind of panicked at the question, considering an honest answer would open up a ton of emotional shit neither of us needed right now. The beast, though, just laughed and shrugged and I was content to let its answer stand.

"That was three, yeah?" David's voice was a little weaker than it had been before. We were nearing the council chamber and it was making him nervous. I couldn't blame the kid, that's for sure…

"That was three." I confirmed. "And the next one will either be more heavily guarded than the last or it will be standing wide open."

"Do I even want to know why they'd leave it open?"

"Because they're a bunch of arrogant fucks that don't think we've got what it takes to see this through."

David didn't say anything else so I didn't either. I kinda wanted to know what was going on in his head but the beast was pretty adamantly against opening up any sort of emotional cans of worms... and, as much as I really hated to agree with it, I figured it was probably right. There was too much at stake.

The door was, as I'd kind of suspected it would be, standing wide open and the corridor itself opened up into a huge round room. There were little rooms off the main room, barely more than alcoves, where the council remained hidden away until they actually had some reason to come together.

The room was empty except for a large table in the center of the room. It was kind of egg-shaped and cut from the same black stone as everything else. It may even have been a single black stone: honestly, it wouldn't have surprised me.

We stood there for a moment while I decided what to do next. I could have called them out. Honestly, things being what they were now, I probably could have commanded they show themselves and had them all on their knees. And while that would have been ten kinds of satisfying, I didn't actually think of it until after I had walked up to the table and stuck the Ubojica into the center of the tabletop.

The blade pierced the stone and the room echoed with a bloodcurdling scream.

It never occurred to me that the stone might be a living thing and, while I really didn't want to hurt any innocent bystanders, I simply didn't care enough to wonder about it at this point.

The scream set off a reaction and there was movement in every doorway: thirteen figures cloaked in darkness emerging from equidistant points around the room.

I felt David's shoulders against mine for a moment then space between us: less than a foot between our backs. No v-shape this time: straight back-to-back. Eyes on the whole room. This was how we'd practiced: how we'd trained to take them on.

And it was on.

"You are trespassing."

I turned toward the voice. A tall thin specter of a being stepped closer. I'd argued with it once before - its name was Sgàil and it kinda hated humans which gave it basically no real reason to be on the council in the first place.

"And you've crossed the wrong line."

"To which line are you referring, McLaren?"

I started to answer but David's voice stopped me. "You know McLaren's dead." Alright, kid. Where are you going with this? "You sent Alex McLaren to their death, didn't you?"

Sgàil turned its attention to David and that sent my defenses into overdrive.

"Thurston? Aren't you supposed to be handling the manticore that's wrapped up in this... mess?"

David shook his head slowly. "You're even stupider than you look."

Another one was moving: a mostly formless being called Paolo.

"Am I?" Sgàil moved closer to David but not yet close enough to strike. Watch yourself, kid. "Am I to believe this *isn't* McLaren?"

It was kind of irksome to get talked around while I was standing right there, but I had an idea where the kid was going and if I popped off with something... well... Alex-like... it would throw a wrench in his plan. I just needed to be patient and make sure Paolo didn't swoop in from the kid's flank.

"If you think this is still McLaren, you're a damned fool." More of them were moving. Whatever you're gonna do, kid, do it quick. "You sent Baron Samedi to kill McLaren but you didn't know who you were targeting." Damn... the kid just threw me for a loop. I'd never been able to identify my nemesis but the kid just dropped Samedi's name like it was common knowledge and, judging from the reactions of some of the council, apparently it was. "You were too stupid to check their bloodline and instead of getting rid of your headache, you woke *Segondè Kochma Wa*."

Sgàil actually took a step back and Paolo slowed its approach.

"You can't be serious."

I didn't realize that was my cue, but apparently the beast was more in tune with the kid at this moment than I was. I leapt to the tabletop and yanked the Ubojica free in one motion just as the kid drew his own blade and turned to bow in my direction. "Your highness."

I roared: it was so deep and loud that the whole damned room shook. The whole fuckin dimension might've shook honestly. I wasn't sure how much of what the kid was spouting was really accurate but it sounded good and it seriously shell-shocked the council.

"*Jumeaux, pitit gason mwen*, your introduction is too kind."

Paolo shrunk away. If I was who the kid said I was and he was who I just said he was, there was no defeating us and Paolo, at least, knew it. Of course, I had no idea if the kid had any connection to Jumeaux or not. It kinda didn't seem likely but it just came out so I ran with it. There was no hesitation, though, when I called him my son. Damn it.

Sgàil was glaring at us both but Paolo had slunk back to join a few others who were, now, visibly distancing themselves from the rest of the council.

"Well, well…"

Finally. Vari had broken her silence.

While the council was, technically, a group of equals it was Vari whose word was ultimately taken as law. Like Šapat before her, Vari was not only the voice of the council but often the only voice of reason in the group. If anyone was going to put an end to this before it got bloody… or whatever it was that the members of the council oozed as they died… it was her.

"Did you bring any other loa with you, Kalfu?" She couldn't be serious. "Or just the human child you've enchanted?"

"The revelation of truth required no enchantment." She didn't seriously think she could accuse me of kidnapping David and that I'd be okay with it. "This body has lost its way, Vari. We are here to set things right."

"That may be true but who are you to decide it, *Segondè Kochma Wa*?"

"You call me by name and ask me that question in the same breath? Has age dulled your wits, Vari?"

"Just trying to understand, *your highness*, exactly what you hope to accomplish here."

If the sarcasm when she said *your highness* wasn't enough to piss me off, the fact that several of the others were trying to move into better fighting positions unnoticed damned sure was. The only reason she opened the dialog was to stall. Dumb bitch.

"Jumeaux?"

"Grandèt ou."

David and I were going to have a very long talk when we got out of this… on several topics. Not only were we going to have to address all the uncomfortable emotional shit, but I really needed to know how he knew so damned much about the *bondye* and when the hell he learned to speak creole.

"What exactly was it that we hoped to accomplish here?"

David smiled and the sparkle in his eye made me pretty damned sure he'd been touched by Jumeaux at the very least. Things just kept getting weirder. "We bring justice, high one."

"That's right. Justice." The beast chuckled. "I keep confusing it with vengeance." My gaze locked on the dark holes sunk in Vari's head. "Vengeance for the lives destroyed by the injustice of this council's directives."

"And yet, you survived," Vari hissed.

The beast roared and the overseers flinched in unison. "Your commands destroyed Alex McLaren." I sprang off the table and prowled the circle, snarling at the overseers as I moved. The kid was still in position: watching carefully, ready to leap to my side at the first sign of trouble. "Your commands destroyed David Thurston." He had to have known I'd go this route because the kid didn't even flinch. "Your commands destroyed Terrence Carlin and his partner." I stopped in front of Vari, my face inches from hers: teeth bared. "And that's just the last two months."

Vari trembled but tried to stand tall.

I leaned in close enough that I could have licked her face if I'd wanted to. I'd be lying if I said the thought didn't cross my mind. "Justice will be served."

"Your arrogance is astounding," Vari whispered, gripping desperately to what was left of her composure with her bony fingers.

I'd wanted to retain some measure of control but there was no way the council was going to be swayed if any part of me showed itself in the confrontation and, judging by Vari's continued challenge, it had. "*Pitit mwen, le lach.*" It was all the warning I could give the kid and I hoped it was enough.

I heard his voice as the beast took over: distant and fading. "*Rekonèt.*"

The beast rose to its full height which, somehow, made it about six inches taller than my actual height but whatever. I wasn't going to question it. Half the overseers dropped to their knees, or whatever passed for them, as it squared its shoulders and roared again. Its language was far more growl and roar than words but I don't think anything in the room had a problem understanding it.

"*Still you defy me?!*" Vari stumbled backward and the beast closed the distance. "*Order my son to kill his own mother and stand there like you've some way to justify your decision?!*"

"You speak in riddles, Imperial," Vari stammered.

"*I speak clear enough for all here to understand.*" Yeah. Even the kid. Thanks, asshole. Way to make sure I can't weasel out of the uncomfortable conversations later.

"The boy is not your…"

"*If blood was of consequence, would this body have chosen McLaren?*"

"I… um…" There it was. The beast had tripped her up: forced her to confirm they'd fucked up when they activated me.

"This body serves the Empire, does it not?"

It had taken me way too long to figure out where the beast was getting its information. It wasn't until now that it even registered. One of the trinkets Coralia had prepared hung on a leather strap around my neck: a worn and tarnished medallion etched with a double-headed eagle. I didn't know if it was a mobile history lesson or a trigger for genetic memories but, either way, it was giving us both what we needed. The council's origins had been shrouded in antiquity but now I knew: it was part of a network of similar bodies established by the barong ket imperial family to maintain control over the worlds.

Councils like this were *how* the barong ket had been able to maintain control. I hated them even more, now.

"The Empire is gone." Vari's voice was weak. Wavering. Almost like she knew what kind of hell she was unleashing.

"As I breathe, so breathes the Empire." The beast flung one arm to identify the room. *"Ask your friends, on their knees, to whom they pledge their allegiance."* It leaned in, knocking Vari's hood from her head, and whispered in her ear. *"It's not you."*

Sgàil, who was one of the few who hadn't fallen to their knees either out of reverence or fear, began moving slowly toward the table where David stood. The beast didn't turn but it didn't need to. The whole room behaved like a single organism and, when the beast claimed dominion, it somehow synced up to its senses. At least, that's my theory.

"Harm one hair on my son's head, Sgàil..."

"And it will be his last act, *paran*," David said, glaring at the shadow now moving away from him.

Another voice entered the conversation. One of the overseers who'd fallen to its knees: a figure shrouded in the layers of robes indicative of ancient desert societies. "Your command, my liege?"

Could it be that easy? After all we'd done to get here, was it possible I could just call them off?

"This body has become corrupt." The beast turned away from Vari and prowled the circle once more. *"Twisted."* It stopped in front of Sgàil. *"Consumed by the very evil that it was called to defend the world against."*

"But the last Emperor..."

The beast's clawed hand snapped out and closed around Sgàil's thin neck. Apparently there was going to be more blood, after all. *"The last Emperor died seven hundred years ago."* I watched as the beast's hand closed tighter but I couldn't bring myself to even try to stop it. These beings had been the puppeteers of my sorrow and responsible for the destruction of so many lives… the kid was right. It was justice. *"If that is where your allegiance lies, then lie with him."*

Sgàil struggled against the beast's hold in an attempt to speak but its head ended up dropping over the beast's hand. It let go and Sgàil's body fell in a misshapen pile on the black stone floor.

"Who among you still stands in challenge to the rule of *Segondè Kochma Wa*?" David's voice echoed against the walls of the chamber.

The few councilmembers who'd remained on their feet sunk slowly to the floor.

All but Vari.

"What have you become, Alex McLaren?" Her voice was soft. Scared.

The beast turned toward her and growled.

David's hand touched my arm. "Spare her, *paran*."

"Why should I?"

"You are greater than they are, your highness," David answered, his voice echoing in the chamber. "They serve you. Let them earn forgiveness."

The beast growled for a moment then, to my surprise (and David's too, I'm pretty sure), nodded slowly. *"This body is dead. Its corpse will burn. If you desire to continue your existence, be certain I never see your face again."*

One dead and an offer of mercy for the rest: maybe I did have a little influence over the beast after all. That or it cares for the kid as much as I do. Either way, the beast was done here and I wasn't about to argue. It turned back toward the corridor and David moved from his place to walk by its side.

By my side.

The beast was fading some: pulling back to that place it had sat since the kid and I had started training. Close enough to augment pretty much everything but leaving me in control. Which made sense, since the beast really was me… but I was still having trouble wrapping my head around it.

David had been silent. Not uncommon but there was something about the silence that concerned me.

"You okay, kid?"

"I felt it."

We kept walking. We needed to be out of the tunnel before I incinerated it.

"Felt it?"

"They… disconnected? I guess?"

I nodded and we kept walking.

I hadn't felt anything but, technically, any actual physical connection they had left would have been severed when I died: the fact that they were still able to use the same physical cues to control me those few times after were because my brain hadn't fully accepted all the changes my death catalyzed.

The first gate was still open and the remaining naga bowed low as we walked through.

The remains of the wooden door and its Hollywood-reject guards were just as we left them.

When we finally reached the conference room, all four of the men who'd been there were gone but the room was still a mess. We stopped together and turned back to look down the tunnel.

"Segondè kochma wa?"

"Wi, pitit gason m'?"

"Will they all die?"

"Those that remain, yes."

He nodded slowly. I was having a hard time reading him.

"You okay with that?"

He nodded a little more firmly. "Yeah, I just... yeah."

"You just what, kid?"

Ideals and conscience. The beast was enough a part of me that it had to know this was coming. The kid was too much like me and, regardless of how justified our actions might be, it still felt a little like murder.

"Yours is the new empire, yeah?"

"Yeah." I let the word drag out. I thought I knew where he was going but I wanted to be sure.

"Well, I mean... if you get to make the rules, then..."

It occurred to me that, no matter what I said, David might not believe it was me and not the beast... which was a totally valid concern and one sparked more pride in me than annoyance. "You want me to show them mercy?"

"It's just that..."

"Done."

"There were only a couple that... wait. Mac? Did you just say done?"

I managed to chuckle just a bit and nodded as I draped my arm around his shoulders. "Yeah, kid. I said done."

"But I..."

"The best parts of me got nothing to do with me, son." Wasn't really planning on starting this conversation in the conference room of the council's public front but whatever. "It's all about the very few people I give a damn about because those people guide my soul." I stepped slightly away, took a deep breath, and turned to face him. "You want me to show these bastards mercy? It's done."

"So, what do we do now?"

"Go home." I shrugged then nodded as my brain worked its way through everything that was happening. "We go pick up Belle and we go home."

I locked the conference room door and pulled it shut behind us. No sense having anyone that didn't belong down there stumbling across the entrance. The gatekeeper looked up when we walked into the office: her face pale, her hands trembling.

"You need to have someone come fix the whiteboard," I told her as we walked by.

David chuckled as we walked to the truck.

"What?"

"Have someone come fix the whiteboard," he laughed. "That's cold, Mac."

We laughed as we climbed into the truck but there was something serious in the corner of his mouth. I could see it. I just couldn't tell what it was.

"What is it, really?"

"What?"

"Something's buggin you."

David took a breath. "It's really noth..."

"Don't say it's nothing." His face scrunched up the same way Belle's did when I interrupted him. "What is it?"

"It's dumb, but... you keep calling me *son*..."

It hit like a gut-punch. How the hell did I do that? Me, of all people? Just popping off with some blatantly gendered...

"No, it's cool," David said quickly. Apparently, he could read me better than I could read him right now. "It's actually... like... really cool, I just... It feels weird to call you Mac all the time but..."

I chuckled, feeling like a weight had been pulled off my chest. "*Paran* fell off your lips pretty easy back there." I shrugged. "And since I don't think this stupid accent is going anywhere anytime soon..."

"Hmm. Belle likes it, doesn't she?" David smirked.

"There's a little more to it than that." I laughed and started the truck.

~23~

We pulled up to the beach house and David looked over at me with a hundred questions behind his eyes. "She's here?"

"Where else would she be?"

"I just thought…" We climbed out of the truck. "…she was… y'know… going *away* away until we…"

"Can you think of a safer place for her than here?"

David laughed. "I guess not."

We walked up the path and I stopped him near the door. "Last time we were here was kind of an emergency rush thing but…" I knelt down and unzipped my boots and nodded toward his shoes. "House rules."

He nodded and knelt beside me to loosen the laces on his shoes. "Guess I probably better learn 'em now, huh, *Par*?"

The way he cut off *paran* and kind of swallowed the r at the end made it sound almost like he called me 'pa.' While it wouldn't have been my first choice and still wasn't really accurate, it was probably one of the better options for most of the surrounding area. "Guess so."

With our shoes on the little rack next to the walk and our sock-covered feet on the last couple paving stones, the door opened and Coralia smiled at us. "What took you so long, Alex?" she chided.

"Sorry, *en peṇ*." I shrugged, leaning forward to kiss her cheek. "Traffic was a bitch."

"And you? David?" She turned toward the kid and leaned forward to kiss his cheek. "Is that your excuse too?"

"Hey, *paran* was driving," he chuckled.

Her eyebrows rose and her smile kind of glowed when he called me *paran*. "Don't," I said quickly. "Just don't."

She laughed as she stepped back and ushered us into the house.

I glanced around the living room, probably a little too anxiously, and heard
Nikolai laugh from the hall. "She is down on the beach." I was already almost at
the back door when I heard his laughter quiet a bit and his invitation to David to
sit and tell them what had happened. In the back of my head, it registered that
Nik called him *onuk* but I couldn't even be irritated that the old man had
automatically accepted David as my son without any sort of actual introduction,
explanation or confirmation.

Belle was standing at the edge of the water with her back to the house.
Alarms rang in the back of my head: the sea was rough and the wind was kind of
wild - there was no way she could hear what might be coming up behind her. I
managed to fight off the urge to lecture her about the dangers, though. Her body
was shaking slightly, her shoulders bouncing as she stared out to sea. It all fell
together in my head: she was standing there sobbing. I broke into a run.

When I was close enough I thought she could hear me, I stopped running.

"I thought I told you, *nanm mwen,*" I called out. "I can't stand to see you cry."

I saw her shoulders straighten and her body tremble as she sucked in a
deep breath before she turned around. I knew she was afraid she was hearing
things: that the sound of my voice on the wind was nothing more than her
imagination trying to console her. When her eyes confirmed what her ears had
heard, though, the fear melted off her face and she started running toward me.
From a distance, it probably looked like every cheesy stereotypical romance
reunion: her hair bouncing as she ran and her dress billowing as she leapt into
my arms. We were a million miles away from your typical fairy tale, sure, but I
damned sure wasn't going to turn down any part of *happily ever after* the
universe decided to give us.

~X~

Late that night, with David passed out in the guest room, Belle curled up next to me on the couch. When the adrenaline that had kept him on his feet finally quit forcing itself into his blood, the kid damned near fell over. It wasn't a surprise, really: except maybe to him. I'd carried him into the guest room and set him on the bed, but Belle had insisted on checking on him and covering him with a blanket.

"Y'know, I called him *son* about a dozen times today," I told her, finally taking a drink from the bottle of whiskey I'd been staring at for the last ten minutes.

She laughed softly. "And how'd that go over?"

"Little shit was calling me *paran* by the time we got back to the beach house." I took another drink.

Belle sat up and looked at me seriously. All the laughter in her eyes was gone: filled with something else I truly couldn't identify. "Mac?"

"He's almost eighteen." I didn't know what she wanted me to say and I wasn't about to try to figure it out. I just had to finish getting my thoughts out. Whatever it was, this was all new ground and she was going to have to help me find our way through it. "And the guest room just sits there empty anyway. We're both gonna live a good long while and his aunt doesn't…" Her expression had softened and her eyes were glistening with tears. I panicked. "What is it, Belle?"

She leaned forward and kissed me softly. "Next time you take Stef flowers, tell her I'll take good care of him."

I set the whiskey bottle on the floor and wrapped my arms around her as she snuggled against me. I didn't bother trying to control the sobs building in my chest and Belle snuggled closer in response to them.

It didn't make any sense to be crying, of course. There was only one part of anything that could even make me sad right now and, with that one statement from Belle, even that wasn't really sad. It was a mixture of relief, I decided, and joy and an overwhelming feeling of contentment.

I finally understood that cliche about the heart being so full it might burst: filled with the love of my beautiful partner, pride in a kid that had somehow become our son who was sleeping a few rooms away, and the knowledge that I was - hands down - the luckiest bastard on the planet.

ABOUT THE AUTHOR

Carrie Baize was born in Santa Rosa and has lived most of her life in California's Central San Joaquin Valley. She graduated from C.L. McLane High School and continued her education at Fresno City College.

She is an avid role player and has spent a great deal of time in a number of fantasy worlds: some well-known and some of her own design.

She credits her parents with her love of the arts and her father, in particular, for her love of role playing and fantasy world creation.

In addition to writing, she regularly spends inordinate amounts of time and energy crocheting, engraving glassware, and cooking.

Carrie is blessed with a family who, although scattered across the United States, are incredibly supportive and truly believe in her ability to make her dreams come true.

She lives in the foothills above Fresno with her husband, daughter, rescue chihuahua, and a shepherd-mix granddog.

ALSO FROM CARRIE BAIZE

The Scarred Sun Trilogy
Dissension
Destiny
Darkness

The Rio Crew Novels
Summer of Blood
The Wolves of Rio Hevrir
The Gardens of Delora Valley
Wonderland

Urban Wardens
Alpha to Oblivion
Crash and Burn

The Heroes of Vadim
Episode I – Into the Mountain
Episode II – Drop Point Disaster

and

Legacy

www.carriebaize.com